Susan Carlisle's love affair with books began when she made a bad grade in mathematics. Not allowed to watch TV until the grade had improved, she filled her time with books. Turning her love of reading into a love for writing romance, she now pens hot Medicals. She loves castles, travelling, afternoon tea, reading voraciously and hearing from her readers. Join her newsletter at SusanCarlisle.com.

PACIFIC PARADISE, SECOND CHANCE

SUSAN CARLISLE

MILLS & BOON

Published in Great Britain 2020
by Mills & Boon, an imprint of HarperCollins*Publishers*
1 London Bridge Street, London, SE1 9GF

© 2020 Susan Carlisle

ISBN: 978-0-263-08788-8

MIX
Paper from
responsible sources
FSC® C007454

This book is produced from independently certified FSC™ paper
to ensure responsible forest management.
For more information visit www.harpercollins.co.uk/green.

Printed and bound in Great Britain
by CPI Group (UK) Ltd, Croydon, CR0 4YY

To Colton

CHAPTER ONE

LANDON COCHRAN, MD, scrolled through the pages of the file on his tablet again. He studied the name in black on the screen: *Macie Beck*. Surely it wasn't the same woman. There must be any number of Macie Becks in the world. What were the chances that the one he had known was currently in the Northern Mariana Islands? Even slimmer the chance that she'd be on the small island of Saipan? It couldn't be her.

As the one-hundred-and-fifty-passenger plane circled the twelve-mile-long lush green island below, Landon looked out the window. Though it was an American territory, Saipan was closer to China than to Hawaii.

The plane lined up for its approach along the single landing strip of the airport, which was built on top of a mountain. This was nothing like the busy airports he was used to. There was none of the hustle and bustle, not even another plane in sight.

He gathered his satchel and hoped his larger bag had made it onto the airplane. In this part of the world, weight was carefully considered on flights. Often bags would be left behind to show up on the next plane, which might be the next day. It had happened to him only once, but ever since, he carried a change of clothes in his smaller bag just in case.

Soon, the plane landed and passengers were dis-
embarking. As Landon stepped out and walked down
the metal stairway that had been rolled to the plane, he
looked at the lush vines and vegetation all around the
area. This part of the world was hot, muggy and rainy.
Welcome to the tropics, he thought. He followed the other
passengers across the tarmac to the low gray terminal.

Landon entered the cool building and waited for his
luggage. Twenty minutes later, with his rolling bag in
hand, he headed out the glass doors to the parking lot,
where the late afternoon heat was offset by a slight ocean
breeze. Across the street stood the abandoned cement
bones of a chain hotel, left unfinished.

He located a man who held a card with his name on it.

"I'm Dr. Cochran."

"Welcome to Saipan." The man gave him a toothy grin
and took his large bag, then led Landon toward a car. "I
am Mario," he said with a slight accent.

While Mario put his bag in the trunk, Landon chose to
sit in the front so he could check out the area. He wasn't
here to be pampered. He had a tough job ahead, and he
needed to familiarize himself with the people and the
island as quickly as possible.

As Mario drove down the winding road toward the
coast, they passed small square houses made of cement
blocks. Many had grassy yards while others were surrounded by dirt spaces filled with chickens. They turned
south up a wider two-lane road that skirted the coastline. Businesses lined the sides of the road, many with
palm trees in front that swirled in the wind. To Landon's
amazement, cars filled the roadway.

For someone who had grown up in the American Midwest, this was a completely different environment. When
he was in the navy, he'd been deployed as far west as

Hawaii, where he had loved the heat, breeze and ocean. Apparently, he would get plenty of that here. That was, if he had a chance to get out of the hospital long enough to appreciate it. He'd come to evaluate the Saipan Hospital and ensure that it received the updates necessary to give the people of Saipan and the surrounding islands the best healthcare possible.

Soon, a white building with windows running across the front came into view. Mario steered the car into the circular drive and stopped under the brick porte cochere.

"Here we are." Mario gave Landon another grin before getting out. Landon followed suit and met him at the rear of the car to pick up his luggage.

"Thank you," he said to the man, then took the handle of his luggage and rolled it behind him through the glass-door entrance.

Inside, the building was cool. A long tile corridor lay before him, and he searched for a sign that would direct him to the administration office. The pharmacy was located to his left and the emergency waiting room entrance to his right, yet he didn't see any directions to Administration, so he continued down the hallway cross an intersection of a hall and continued on. At the end of the long hall he took a chance and turned left. There he found the office.

After opening the single glass door, he spoke to the thirtysomething, slim, local woman behind the desk. "I'm Dr. Landon Cochran of the World Health Organization. Macie Beck should be expecting me."

Once more, the idea that it might be the same Macie he had known sent a jolt of apprehension through him. Their final parting wasn't one he was proud of. He'd left her in her bed after a night of passion with the promise to call her when he got off his shift at the hospital, but that hadn't happened.

The receptionist glanced toward a closed door. "Macie isn't here right now."

"I assume she is expecting me?"

"She was…uh…is, but they were short of help in the ER and she's down there." The woman looked unsure as she picked up the phone. "I'll let her know you're here."

Landon shook his head. "Don't interrupt her if she's working."

Relief replaced the worry in the receptionist's expression. She stood and came around the desk. "Your office is this way." She led him to a doorway across the waiting room area. "Please make yourself at home." She then left Landon to himself.

Landon grabbed his luggage and entered the room. It was a small space by usual office standards, but it suited him. His work as interim administrator of the Saipan Hospital didn't require a grand office. A bookcase with a few items on it filled the wall behind a very basic desk and chair that faced the door. Windows flanked it on both sides. A couple of chairs that didn't look comfortable sat in front of the desk. A small door off to the side led, Landon assumed, to the restroom.

The receptionist returned shortly and said, "I spoke to Macie. She said she would be here as soon as she could get away and for me to help you in any way I can."

"Okay, then let's start with your name." Landon parked his suitcase beside the desk and walked behind it.

"I'm Tatiana Yuka."

He smiled and the woman visibly relaxed. "It's nice to meet you."

"You too, sir. Would you like me to show you around?"

Rolling his chair out, he took his suit jacket off and

hung it over the back. "I think I'd like to see the policy-and-procedures manual first."

"You'll find it right there." She pointed to a thick white notebook on the shelf behind the desk.

He pulled it off the shelf and had a seat. "Thanks. Please let me know when Ms. Beck arrives."

"Yes, sir."

Landon got to work. If all went well with this assignment, that promotion he had been working toward for years would be his. He glanced up to see a couple of hours had passed and still no Macie Beck. It was time to go after her. People didn't usually leave him hanging when he wanted to see them. He stepped out of the office. "Tatiana?"

"Sir?"

"If I'm needed, I'll be in the ER."

Concern washed over her face. "Yes, sir. You know where it is?"

"I do. I saw the sign on the way in." Landon turned right and soon reached the intersection and started up the long hall toward the front of the hospital. This time he observed the areas that made up the hospital more closely. He walked by rooms on each side of the hall. Those appeared to hold general medicine patients. He nodded to staff and people he passed. They all gave him a curious look.

Returning to the first intersection where a similar hall crossed, he stopped and looked down each one. The signs indicated the left hall was the pediatric unit and the other side the geriatric unit. He continued on until he saw the double sliding doors of the emergency room waiting area. As he did, the wail of an ambulance in the distance caught his ear.

He entered the waiting area and spoke to the man behind the registration desk. "Please point me in the direction of Macie Beck?"

The staff member looked uncertain. "Uh, she's busy right now."

Landon's patience had become short. After all, Macie had known when he was arriving at Saipan, and it had been over two hours since she'd been informed that he'd wanted to see her. It was time to search her out. "I think she can take a moment for me. I'm the interim administrator, Dr. Cochran."

The man's eyes widened and he pointed behind him. "Uh...hello, sir. Let me walk back there with you." Landon followed the man through the doors into a large space subdivided into smaller areas by curtains. A circular desk was in the center of the room. In front of it stood a petite woman wearing the same light green scrubs as the rest of the staff. Her back was to him and he could see that her dark brown hair had been pulled back at the nape of her neck.

His heart thumped against his chest wall. He recognized those fine feminine curves. It was *his* Macie Beck.

She turned and her gaze met his.

Of all the islands in all the world, this was the one he'd been assigned to. Now he knew how Rick felt in *Casablanca* when Ilsa showed up in his bar.

Well, well, well. If it wasn't *the* Landon Cochran.

The one who had left her high and dry all those years ago when she'd been working in Hawaii at the Veterans' Hospital. Even a Dear John would have been better than the nothing she got after their one and only night together. Landon had not just ignored her, he had left the island. He'd stamped her "men can't be trusted" card and then disappeared.

To make the situation worse, she had been vulnerable after what had happened with her father, and Landon's defection had devastated her. Her fragile pride had taken another hit. It had taken weeks of them working together for her to start trusting Landon. She didn't have any faith in her judgment regarding people, but Landon had managed to get around that. When he had left, she'd been confident he'd found out what her father had done and wanted nothing more to do with her. Landon wouldn't have been the first person. She had hoped Hawaii would have been far enough away to get out from under her father's criminal shadow.

But that had all been eight years ago. Mercy, Landon still looked good. Handsome as ever. He'd filled out some from the lean young man he had once been. His shoulders seemed broader and his body sturdier. Yet there was something granite hard about him, as if he'd seen some tough times. His hair, a tawny color, still had a touch of the unruly waves she remembered well.

He brushed a hand through it. That was the same gentle hand she had seen in action with patients and had experienced directly when it cupped her cheek just before he'd kissed her. And then had done more. Those thoughts were better off not being revisited.

The siren grew louder, cutting her Landon-induced stupor short. She shook her head. There wasn't time for those memories. "Dr. Cochran, I hope you haven't forgotten your medical skills while pushing papers. We could use them now. Auto accident. Three casualties, one a child."

Macie hurried toward the ER entrance. She didn't have time to worry about Landon. There were patients coming in. As she passed the supply cart, she snatched up a mask and nitrile gloves. She handed Landon a gown and left him to get the other supplies he needed.

"Put the boy in exam room two and the man in three. The woman in six." She followed the gurney with the boy on it.

Macie carried out the processes to hook the boy up to the monitors. A deep voice she had heard for months, maybe even years, after her heart had been broken said, "What do we have here?"

"Eight-year-old boy with lacerations to his leg, face and hand."

Landon stood beside her. Too close. "Before I start stitching, I need X-rays to check for broken bones. Start an IV of fluids and give pain meds as needed. A little something to calm him as well."

"He'll need to go down to X-Ray." Macie punched buttons, getting the monitors set.

Landon asked over his shoulder as he stepped out of the way. "Where's the portable one?"

She hated to admit this. "We don't have one."

"Just see it's done while I check to see if the ER doctor needs help with the other two patients." Landon left her.

Macie saw to the medicines Landon had ordered all the while reassuring the boy that his mother was fine. She then started cleaning around his injuries Landon returned fifteen minutes later.

"Has he been to X-Ray yet?"

"No. They're backed up." Macie continued her work.

Landon's lips thinned into a tight line. "Unhook him. Grab the end of his bed and the IV pole."

"What're we doing?" Macie demanded as she obeyed.

"We're taking him there ourselves."

She couldn't agree with him more. As a nurse practi-

tioner she had authority, but she couldn't override pro-
cedure like Landon was doing. "Yes, sir."

She remembered his curt decisiveness from long ago.
Time hadn't softened that part of his personality. She had
appreciated it back then and did now as well. So why
hadn't he said goodbye to her all those years ago? That
seemed so out of character for him.

Together they rolled the boy out of the department
and into the hallway.

"Which way?" Landon asked over his shoulder as he
pulled the gurney ahead of her.

"Right," she called. "Down the hall on the right."

Moments later they wheeled the boy into X-Ray.

Landon spoke to the woman behind the desk. "This
patient needs X-rays right now."

The woman blinked and stood. "You can't come in
here—"

Oh, no. This wasn't going to go well. Landon was
about to butt heads with Yuri, the most formidable
woman at the hospital. Macie shook her head from where
she stood behind Landon.

"I'm Dr. Cochran. This child needs X-rays before I
can stitch him up. He needs them now."

"Yuri?" Macie gained the woman's attention. "Dr.
Cochran is our new administrator."

Her eyes widened. "Come on through. A clerk was
just on his way to get the boy."

"We have saved him the trouble," Landon said on their
way past her desk. "Macie and I can handle everything."

Minutes later they had the boy on the X-ray table.
Macie stayed with the child as Landon saw to taking the
pictures. When they finished, he studied the film for a
few minutes.

He rejoined them at the gurney and smiled, cheerfully informing the boy, "It looks like there are no broken bones."

"That's good news." Macie patted the boy's shoulder.

"Now we can get you back to the ER. Then you can check on your mother."

The boy nodded, tears welling in his eyes.

Macie pulled the gurney and Landon pushed. "Don't worry, honey. Dr. Cochran is going to take good care of you." She glanced up to see Landon watching them before he looked away to navigate the hallway. She'd forgotten how good he was with people. His smooth charm had certainly gotten to her. Maybe it was because he had recognized the pain in her like he did in his patients.

She'd been a mess back then. The year before, she had learned that her father, whom she had idolized, was a crook. She had lived a charmed life. The big house, the best schools, her first car a sports car. Her family had traveled. Her mother had been on a number of fundraising committees, and she and her brother and sister had run with the "in crowd." Life had been all she could have dreamed of until…it wasn't. It had all been a lie. Her father had built it all on nothing real. When her world had imploded, it had been public and in royal fashion. Her pain had been raw. If Landon hadn't seen it, maybe he had sensed it.

Back at the exam room, she and Landon situated the boy in the right spot.

"I'm going to start with your leg." He spoke to her and the boy. "Then do your head and then your hand. None of this will hurt, I promise. But I'm going to need you to be very still."

The boy nodded as his eyes closed. The pain medicines were taking effect.

"I need a suture kit over here," Landon called to no one in particular as he pulled a stool up next to the bed.

Macie had already anticipated what he would need and had pulled it off the supply cart. Landon began his careful work.

Half an hour later, Macie regarded Landon's patient. "I see you haven't lost your skills."

Landon pushed back from the gurney. He arched his back, stretching. It pulled his dress shirt tight across his chest. The muscles beneath the thin material showed clearly. He straightened and stood, moving to the boy's head. "Let's see about that when I'm completely done here. One down and two to go. At least this one will be in his hairline. He won't have to worry about a scar."

Macie had already cleaned up the last suture kit and replaced it with a new one.

"And I see that you're still as efficient as ever," Landon said.

"I wasn't sure you remembered me." She sucked in a breath, horrified. "I can't believe I just said that. This isn't the time or the place."

"Macie—"

Thankfully, one of the nurses stuck her head inside the room. "Macie, the mother is asking after her son."

Grateful for a reason to escape Landon, Macie said, "Liz, assist Dr. Cochran while I go talk to her."

It was an hour later before she saw Landon again. She'd just hung up the phone after making sure the rooms for the car-accident patients were ready. Her hands shook as he stepped to her.

"If everything is under control here, Macie, we still need to talk."

"Talk?" The word came out as a squawk. She didn't

want to talk about what had happened between them years ago.

"Yes, about the hospital. You are head of Nursing and I'm the interim administrator." He watched her as if he wasn't sure she was understanding him.

Relief settled over her. She could handle business talk. Staying away from the personal was her plan, despite her one little slipup. Still, she couldn't help but want to know why he'd left her like he had. She'd believed that he had enjoyed their night together as much as she had. She had thought they'd had something special. At least, it had been special to her. Even now he made her blood flow faster. She needed a calm head before she discussed anything—including business—with him.

"I've been on for over sixteen hours. What I need right now is a little R & R. Surely our talk can wait until tomorrow. I still need to show you where you're staying while you're here."

"Okay, we'll let the discussion wait. For now. I could use some rest as well."

"Then I'll drive you to your house and we'll meet tomorrow. I have to go by my office, and I can meet you at the front door in ten minutes." That would give her a few more minutes to gather her thoughts.

"I need to get my suitcase. It's in my office. I'll walk with you."

It looked like she wouldn't be getting those sorely needed few minutes alone. As they headed for Landon's office, she nodded back the way they had come. "Thanks for stepping in back there."

His pace matched hers. "Not a problem. I haven't felt that adrenaline rush in a long time."

"How long have you been working for World Health?"

Landon looked at her. "I was given the opportunity about four years ago. And I'm not a paper pusher."

"Hatchet man?"

His brows drew together. "No. Why would you think that?"

"Isn't that what you do? Close hospitals?" She tried to keep her tone light but missed the mark.

"Again, no. I'm here to evaluate the Saipan Hospital. Review what needs to be done to make it better. See what I can do to move it forward. Closing it has never been on the table."

At least that sounded positive. Macie had come to love this island and its people, and she wouldn't let anything hurt them if she could help it. Landon had said all the right things. She hoped he was being honest rather than diplomatic.

"You do know we've had four administrators in as many years."

"I do. I plan to position the hospital and get it the funding it needs, so that a permanent administrator will want to come and stay."

"So, you're swooping in like Superman to make it all better." Now her bitterness had started to show. That wouldn't be the best way to influence Landon.

They had arrived at their offices. "Why, Macie, I never imagined you'd become a cynic. I'm sorry to hear that. I'm not Superman, but I was assigned this job because the World Health board believed I could do some good here."

"I'm not cynical. I'm practical. I'll meet you at the front door." She left him for the safety of her office, where she closed the door.

Thirty minutes later, with Landon in the passenger seat of her car, she drove along the winding road on the opposite side of the island from the hospital. This area wasn't nearly as populated and the road rose high above the water.

Abruptly, he confessed, "I wondered if it was you when I saw your name in the hospital files. I'll admit I'm surprised to find you still this far from the mainland."

Macie glanced at Landon. She'd guessed he had been as surprised to see her as she had been to see him. In a tight tone she answered, "And I imagine you never planned on seeing me again anywhere."

"That's not what I meant. I realize I left in the wrong way." He shifted his long legs in the cramped car.

His discomfort made her smile with satisfaction. Yeah, he'd left in the wrong way. To promise to call a woman you just bedded and not to do so made him the lowest form of male. Even lower than her father had been. She should've known better than to trust the charming Dr. Cochran. That was what her father had done to all those people he'd stolen from. He'd charmed them out of their money like Landon had charmed her into giving herself to him. Back then she'd been too weak to recognize she was being used.

Things were different now. She'd been hurt and had recovered, had learned her lesson. It was time to move on, just like she had worked to do where her father was concerned. "We both have a job to oversee here. Let's focus on that."

"Agreed." He twisted in the seat again. "I think I would've been better off riding strapped to the top. Is this the smallest car ever made?"

Macie chuckled without sympathy. "Pretty much. Keep in mind this is an island and everything must be shipped in. Size matters."

"Got it. No big SUVs."

"A few, but mostly for the tourists." To her great relief his bungalow came into sight. She pulled the car into a short drive and stopped behind another small car. This house had one of the best views on the entire island. It was home for all the hospital administrators, permanent or interim. She'd been there more than once for a social gathering. The porch, with its white wicker rockers and swing, was her favorite. She'd always thought it would be a wonderful spot to sleep on a rainy night. No doubt that would be lost on Landon. He was here for business and nothing more.

The house was situated on a cliff and built out of cinder block like so many of the other homes on Saipan. Coming from a wood-and-brick world, the construction was unusual to her, but she'd soon learned that with the tropical weather and salt water, it was more practical. Surrounding the house was a small grassy yard and on either side of the front door were flowerpots with bright yellow bougainvillea.

She climbed out. Landon did as well with a groan. "Thanks for the torture-chamber ride."

"Would you have rather walked?" she asked too sweetly.

"No. I was thinking more about calling Mario."

Closing the door of the car, she headed toward the house. "You'd still be waiting on him. It's dinner time and he's with his family. Come on, I'll show you around, then I must get going."

He pulled his bag from the back seat. "Where do you live?"

"Close to the hospital." Macie fished for the key to the place in her scrubs pocket and unlocked the door. Pushing it open, she flipped on the overhead light and moved on into the living area, which ran the length of the back of the house. Thankfully, it was maintained and kept furnished in readiness all the time.

Landon put his bag and satchel inside the door and followed her.

"The bedrooms are through there." She pointed down a short hall. "And the kitchen is over this way." She walked to the black-and-white tiled floor. The house was clearly meant for a family.

"This is far more than I need."

Macie agreed with him. "Perhaps, but this is where the administrators live. They hold a certain position on the island. Need to entertain." She moved to the French doors that opened off the living room and stepped out onto the screened porch. Taking a deep breath, she looked out over the rocky cliffs at the bright, lush vegetation to the blue-green ocean beyond. The sight always awed her, making her problems feel small.

She felt more than saw Landon come to stand beside her.

"This is magnificent."

It was nice to hear that he appreciated it. "I couldn't agree more. When someone asks why I live so far from civilization, I describe this view."

"Why *do* you live so far from civilization?"

Macie had no interest in talking with him or with anyone else about why she had run away to the islands. She wanted to forget that time. That was her secret to carry. She had no desire to relive those days. Seeing him again was enough emotional upheaval for one day.

Landon shifted beside her. "Sorry. That's really not my business."

On that they could agree. She turned and started toward the door. "I'll see you tomorrow, Dr. Cochran. The keys to your car are on the hook by the door. If you need anything, call the hospital. They can get in touch with me. I'll send someone."

He muttered a bewildered "Okay."

It wasn't until she'd backed out of the drive and headed down the road that she took a few deep breaths and settled her racing mind. As if it wasn't bad enough to have Landon back in her life, he'd done the double whammy by bringing up thoughts of her father. Somehow, every truly painful event in her life had been crammed into today.

CHAPTER TWO

LANDON HAD BEEN behind his desk working for a couple of hours when he glanced up to see Macie headed for her office. He looked at his watch. Seven o'clock. She hadn't slept in either.

He needed to move this review along. If he could implement some big-impact, low-cost innovations, that would secure him the job he really wanted— Director of the World Health Organization. His focus was improving medical conditions in underprivileged and sparsely populated areas. He could proudly say he had been successful. The Saipan Hospital shouldn't be any different.

He walked over to Macie's door and leaned his shoulder against the frame.

She looked up. He hadn't forgotten just how attractive she was. When they had first met at the hospital where they'd worked on the same floor, she had struck him has a pretty woman, but she'd had such sad eyes.

After working together for a few weeks, they both happened to attend the party of a coworker where they had gravitated toward each other, spending most of their time in a corner talking. Since the party had been held in the apartment complex where they both lived, he had walked her home.

On an impulse, he had asked her out and they'd dated

over the next month as their schedules had allowed. One thing had led to another and she had invited him into her bedroom. With Macie he had always felt a special spark. That hadn't gone away.

Landon looked at her closer. That sadness she'd once had in her eyes was gone now. Was it defiance, determination or maybe unease that had replaced it? The last bothered him more than he liked.

She cleared her throat.

He blinked and straightened. "Do you mind if we have our talk over some food? I'm hungry."

That didn't seem to reassure her. "Shouldn't we do it privately?"

"I don't think what we say at this point will be so sensitive we need to worry. We aren't going to get into a public brawl, are we?"

"I don't know. I've not heard what you have to say yet."

He liked this frank Macie. She'd been so meek and unsure when he'd first met her that she would have never spoken to him like that. Maybe he needed to ease his way in more, get her on his side. "I'm more interested in what you think needs to be done."

Her eyes widened. "I do have some ideas."

"I thought you might." He nodded.

She leveled a look at him. "You don't know me well enough now to know what I'd think."

"Touché. And that may be so, but I saw your determination in the ER and your face when you had to tell me there was no portable X-ray machine. I'm making an educated guess that you have some thoughts on what could improve care around here."

Her lips thinned in thought.

He waved a hand encouraging her in his direction. "Come on, live dangerously and have breakfast with me."

She hesitated a moment before she pushed the chair back and stood. He didn't let the satisfaction show on his face for fear she would change her mind. Macie would be a key component in the success of his job here. Somehow, he had to win her over.

Macie led the way out of her office, turned left down the hall and headed through a breezeway. "I see you found your way to the hospital this morning."

He matched his strides to her shorter ones. "I did. I made a couple of wrong turns but I managed."

"The nice thing about living on an island is if you keep going in one direction you'll eventually end up where you need to be." She opened a door and they entered another building, which held the cafeteria.

There they went through the line and chose their food. Macie directed him into a courtyard filled with palm trees and cement tables with benches.

Landon set his tray on the table. "This is nice. I don't usually get to eat a meal in such nice weather."

She sat down across from him. "One of the perks of living so close to the equator. It's warm year-round. We have the steadiest temperature in the world, I've been told."

They ate for a few minutes before Macie said, "So what're you wanting to do here, Landon? Save us from ourselves?"

He gave her a level look. "I don't think you're coming into this with the right attitude."

"The only attitude I have is one of skepticism. I've seen administrators come in here and think they can change the world, then they leave. 'Fix-it guys' don't last. No one ever stays long enough to see through even one change. What this hospital needs is someone who'll stay for the long haul. Those of us left behind just keep on doing what we can, doing what we know is best for our patients."

"I get it. We need to make it attractive for an administrator to stay. I'll put that at the top of the list."

She put her fork down and leaned forward. "If you're making a list—"

"I can assure you I am." He forked up some eggs and looked at her.

"Then we need equipment. More specifically, money for it." She almost spat the words.

"Okay. I'll add that to the list." He continued to watch her. That was something he had always enjoyed doing. Her face was so expressive. Especially that moment when he had entered her. After all these years he could remember it clearly. Landon shook his head, clearing it of those types of thoughts.

"And we need doctors who specialize but who are also willing to do general medicine." Macie's words came faster.

"Okay."

She leaned toward him in her eagerness. "There need to be incentives so that they stay for an extended length of time."

"Anything more?"

Macie pursed her lips and leaned back. "I think that's it for right now."

He nodded. "Feel better?"

She smiled. "As a matter of fact, I do."

Landon continued, "I've been reviewing protocols, staff positions and the number of employees. I believe there are areas that can be improved. I'd like us to sit down and evaluate each department individually. I'd also like your insights on each of them."

"Okay. And when do you expect me to do my job?"

"Don't you have someone you can call on to help?" She wasn't going to make this easy on him. He didn't want to have to pull rank to get her cooperation.

"I might, but they have their jobs as well." She pushed her tray away and folded her arms on the table, pinning him with a look. She should have asked this yesterday in the ER."You do have a current medical license?"

"I do."

"Then I'll tell you what. Why don't you take a few days to work in every department and get some first-hand knowledge instead of looking through the numbers? Then you might really get to know what's going on. We're short on help and you could do something that would actually matter while you're here."

Apparently, the soft-spoken woman he remembered was long gone. Macie wanted to play hardball. She continued to watch him intently. He had never felt more like a nasty germ under a microscope. "You know, that's not a bad idea. But only if you're working right beside me."

She blinked. Her mouth opened and closed. "Why do I need to do that?"

"Because you know everyone, and they'll be less on their guard around me with you putting them at ease."

That determined look had turned to one of anxiousness. "But I can't—"

"Sure you can. Plan our schedule." He checked his watch. Standing, he picked up his tray and hers as well. "I'll be ready to start tomorrow. Have a good day, Macie."

Landon turned his back to her with the sting of daggers hitting him between the shoulder blades. He didn't have to see Macie to know she wasn't happy with him.

Macie watched Landon stroll off like his demands hadn't twisted her world into a knot. He'd called her bluff and now she'd be stuck working closely with him for the fore-seeable future. This wasn't what she wanted. All that planning she'd done the night before to stay as far away from him as possible had just gone up like steam after a rain.

She wanted the best for the hospital, and was willing to do what she could to help that happen, but working every minute with Landon might be more than she could endure. The hospital board had requested she be the point person between the hospital and the World Health Organization when the Board had asked for help in developing a strategy. When she agreed to the role, she'd had no idea Landon would be the person she'd have to work with.

For her, their past was just too tender. She would have said that she was over it until Landon had shown up. His arrival had brought all those emotions rushing back.

Only a few months before she'd first met Landon, she had joined a traveling nurses program to get away from the media, who were hounding her about her father's Ponzi scheme bilking millions of people out of their savings. Her family had lived in luxury while others were being cheated. To think about it even now made her sick.

Being on the other side of the world had been the perfect way to get out of the spotlight. The Veterans' Hospital in Hawaii had been her first assignment. She hadn't trusted anyone, yet the new navy doctor, Landon Cochran, had gotten past her defenses—at least those around her heart. She had started to trust again. Not enough to share everything about her past but enough to enjoy his warmth. She had started to believe there could be something real and lasting between them.

Then when he hadn't called, when he'd just disap-peared, she'd felt used. Just like when her father had de-manded she attend his trial and stand behind him at all the media events. It wasn't surprising Landon's actions had knocked her feet out from under her again. She was obviously a poor judge of character. Never again would she put herself in the position to let someone do that to her.

It wasn't until she had been assigned to Saipan that she had started rebuilding her life. When it had been time to move on to a new location, she had decided to leave the traveling nurses program and had stayed in Saipan. Here she could make a difference, and no one knew who her father was. Her work became her life. There had been a man here and there but nothing that meant anything.

Macie slowly walked back to her office. The hallways were busier than they had been an hour earlier. She stopped a couple of times to answer people's questions. When she finally arrived at Administration, Landon's door was closed. Was he out somewhere checking on things or cloistered with his papers? It didn't matter. She had to figure out their schedule, including making arrangements with the other departments for them to fill in. Then she had to find someone to cover her job. Easier said than done. Her guess was that she'd be putting in extra hours for the next few weeks.

As she came in and out of her office throughout the day, Landon's door remained closed. Before she left for the evening, she knocked on it.

"Enter." Landon's deep voice came from the other side. She'd secretly hoped that he wouldn't answer and she could just leave the scrubs she'd brought on his desk.

She opened the door to find him sitting behind the desk with notebooks and papers spread out all over it. Landon looked up. He wore black-rimmed glasses that should have distracted from his looks; instead, they made him appear super sexy. She stared.

"Hey, what's up?"

Her attention went to his dress shirt sleeves, which were once again rolled up to reveal tan forearms. His hair looked as if he'd been running his hands through it.

"Macie?"

"Oh, I brought you some scrubs. You might want to wear them. You stand out like a flower in the desert in your dress clothes. If you haven't noticed, we're more casual on the island."

"Like a flower in the desert, huh? A flower on a cactus, I'd guess."

"You said that, not me." She grinned and stepped closer to the desk, holding up the garments.

"Why just green scrubs?"

"I don't know. It's what they were wearing when I first came to the hospital. I think everyone sees it as a team uniform."

"A team? Interesting. I can use that to my advantage."

Macie didn't like his look or his statement. She was tempted to snatch the clothing back. "What do you mean by that?"

He stretched his arms over his shoulders. "Just that I've learned that my job doesn't encourage people to open up, and I need them to."

She watched his shirt tighten across his chest. He'd taken care of himself through the years. "I don't imagine it does. Do you mind that?"

He shrugged. "It's more like, I accept it comes with the territory."

"Then why do what you do?"

He crossed his arms on his desk. "Because it needs to be done and I'm good at it."

"You like being a hatchet man?" She couldn't keep her distaste out of her words.

"I'm not a hatchet man." He enunciated each word. "I'd like you to quit looking at me like that. Because it isn't true. I'm good at ferreting out problems and offering solutions."

"And you like that better than caring for people?" Disbelief rang clear in her voice.

"I am still caring for people. Just not one at a time."

She shoved the scrubs at him. "Speaking of one at a time, we're expected on the floor at seven a.m."

Landon's voice followed her to the door. "I'll be ready to get started when you are."

How sad was it that she liked that deep throaty sound of his voice as much as she had before?

The next morning, Macie looked up to see Landon standing in her doorway wearing the scrubs. He made the less than attractive clothes look dashing and, worse than that, the color of them brought out the green in his eyes. She had to figure out some way to wall off the pull he had on her if she were to survive his stay. His hopefully short-lived stay.

"I'm ready." She stood and came around the desk, picking up her phone as she went.

"So where are we headed?" Landon asked as she joined him.

"We'll be spending the next two days in the geriatric unit."

He waved an arm toward the door. "Great. Lead on."

To her amazement, he didn't seem deterred. All he did was wrap the stethoscope he had been holding around his neck and head toward the door. She hadn't expected enthusiasm.

Macie led the way to their assigned area. Stopping at the nurses' desk, she checked in and introduced Landon to the two nurses there. Taking the handle of the chart cart, she pushed it toward the closest patient room.

"What're you doing?"

"Making rounds."

"With that?" He waved a hand toward the cart. "I've not seen a chart cart except in pictures. Don't you have a tablet to do charting on?"

She shook her head. "They are on the wish list but there hasn't been enough money to make that happen."

He shook his head but didn't say anything more as they stopped outside a patient's room.

Macie pulled a chart out of the rack and flipped it open.

"So tell me about our first patient."

"This is Mrs. Neeboo. She's eighty-four years old. Has COPD. She had a heart attack twenty years ago but has done well since. I think at last count she has ten grand-children and eight great-grandchildren."

Landon's brow wrinkled and he stepped closer, look-ing over her shoulder at the chart. His scent filled her nose. He smelled of citrus and something else she knew all too well was special to him. Macie still liked it. Too much.

"Is that thing about her grandchildren written on the chart?"

She grinned. "No. I just know that. A couple of her children and three of her grandchildren work here at the hospital."

His lips thinned into a tight smile. "Funny. I was won-dering what was being required for your records."

"This hospital is very much a family affair. Many families depend on it not only for their medical care but also for their livelihood."

"Point taken, Macie." He took the chart from her.

Macie knocked on the door, then pushed it open. She went to the end of the bed and Landon joined her. From there the aging woman could clearly see them.

"Good morning, Mrs. Neeboo," Macie said. "How're you feeling today?"

"Much better. I'm ready to go home. My family is expecting me to cook Sunday dinner."

Macie glanced at Landon, who was reading the chart. "Mrs. Neeboo, this is Dr. Cochran. He'll be taking care of you today."

The older woman gave him her attention. A suspicious look filled her eyes. The island people were friendly, but they also guarded themselves until they knew people well.

Landon handed the chart back to Macie and stepped to the side of the bed. In a gentle voice he said, "Mrs. Neeboo, it's nice to meet you. Please call me Landon. I'd like your permission to examine you. I promise to be gentle."

Macie moved so she stood across from him.

"Now, I'm going to have to shine a light in your eyes."

Landon pulled a penlight out of his pocket. He had come prepared. I know it's irritating but it gives me an idea of how you're doing. I'd like you to look up at the TV and keep looking that way." He shone the light in both her eyes. "Good, good." He flipped off the light and slipped it back into his pocket. "Now I'd like you to watch my finger." He moved it back and forth.

Mrs. Neeboo did as he asked with great concentration.

"Good. This might tickle a little bit, but I'm going to check your ears."

He pulled an otoscope out of his pocket and placed it in the woman's ears.

"Please put your head back."

Mrs. Neeboo did as he asked and Landon looked up her nostrils.

"Perfect."

He pulled his stethoscope from around his neck, put the ear pieces in and placed the bell on the woman's chest. "I need to give your heart a good listen."

Macie watched Landon's face as he focused on what he heard. His gaze flickered to hers. That hot awareness she remembered from before zipped through her.

Landon said to Mrs. Neeboo, "Wonderful. Could I get you to sit forward a little?"

He slipped his arm in behind her to help. Macie supported her as well.

"Breathe deeply for me." Landon moved the bell to the patient's back.

The old woman did as he asked.

"One more time please." He paused, then said, "Very nice." His arm brushed Macie's as he eased it out and Mrs. Neeboo lay back.

Even such a small touch was like hot lava against her skin. She couldn't afford to have that type of reaction where Landon was concerned.

"I'm going to do some poking and prodding. Just let me know if anything hurts." Landon started at her neck and worked over her shoulders. "Now I'm going to have to push on your abdomen, so bear with me."

Macie slowly lowered the bed so the older woman was lying flat.

"Tell me about the people in all these pictures." Landon glanced at the frames lining the counter under the window.

"My grandchildren." There was a proud note in her voice. "They are blessings from God. Do you have any children, Dr. Cochran?"

Landon continued to work as he answered, "No. Not even a wife."

Why did that bit of knowledge make Macie's heart skip?

Mrs. Neeboo patted Landon's forearm. "Life is too short to live it alone."

"Maybe one day..." Landon sounded as if he were placating the woman, trying to get out of the discussion.

Macie would have found it humorous if she hadn't been so interested in his answers. Which she shouldn't be. Why hadn't he married?

"All is well. Next, I'd like to have a little peek at your legs and feet." Instead of flipping the sheet down, he carefully pushed it up from her feet. He then gently ran his hands up her calves. Smiling, he placed the sheet back. "You seem to be in good form."

Mrs. Neeboo looked at Landon as if he were a piece of candy. He'd charmed the old woman, just like he'd once charmed Macie. But that wouldn't happen again. Macie adjusted the blanket over the patient.

"I think, the rate you're going, you should be home for that Sunday dinner." He patted her hand. "But I don't want you doing the cooking. Take a few days to be waited on. It was nice to meet you. I look forward to seeing you outside the hospital instead of in it. I'm going to write up your discharge order soon. One of the nurses will be in to see about getting you out of here."

"Thank you, doctor."

Landon patted her leg. "You're welcome."

Once again in the hall, he turned to Macie and put out his hand. "Next."

Macie handed him another chart then followed him to the next patient's door. She couldn't deny that Landon had done a fine job with Mrs. Neeboo. Everything about his interactions with their patient had been genuinely caring and concerned. Macie wasn't surprised, but it would have been nice if she could have found some fault in him. He was almost too good to be true.

Landon had forgotten what it was like to work on a hospital floor. It had taken him hours of examinations to finish these rounds. He'd become rusty. Now he still had more hours of dictation to update the charts. As he and Macie had seen patients, he had noticed the other nurses going in and out of the rooms. He'd been impressed with the staff in the geriatric ward by the end of the day.

The only thing he found lacking was electronic records. He didn't like admitting it, but Macie's demand that he work on the floors was starting to pay off in a huge way. Nowhere in the paperwork of the hospital had he read that there was a need for electronic records. How the last administrator had failed to place them in the budget he had no idea. Was that because it was so far down on the list of needs that it hadn't made it on to the list?

For the rest of the week, his days continued much like the first one. He found he actually looked forward to the weekend. At least he could sleep in. Yet there would be still more paperwork to review.

When he left the hospital on Friday night, Macie wasn't in her office. He assumed she had already gone for the day. While they were seeing patients, she had also been on the phone handling any problems that had arisen. He'd not seen her lose her temper even once, and he was impressed.

With his bag filled with papers he planned to review over the weekend, he exited the hospital. The smell of rain hung heavy in the air. This was the tropics after all.

Showers were part of everyday life. They came and went just as quickly; few lingered for any length of time.

He'd be glad to get home to put his feet up. He'd been on them far more than he was used to. Still, it had been a rewarding week. Getting out from behind a desk and using his knowledge and skills had felt good. He and Macie had made a great team.

After pulling the small car, which was thankfully larger than Macie's, into the carport beside his house, he climbed out. He couldn't think of the last time he'd had a real home. Maybe before his father had left. After that it had been apartments, military housing and hotels—nothing permanent. He found he rather liked coming home to his bungalow on the cliff. He particularly enjoyed the porch. If he wasn't careful, he'd burn hours watching the ocean roll in as the sun reflected across the water.

Saturday midmorning he drove to the hospital to pick up more material to review. A number of staff spoke to him as he walked down the hall. He had no doubt that was because they had seen him with Macie during the week. She'd given him the seal of acceptance.

He entered the administration area and noticed Macie's office door was open. She sat behind her desk, her attention on something in front of her.

"What're you doing here?" Landon hadn't meant for the question to sound like an accusation. He was just surprised to see her. He went to stand in her doorway.

Macie's head jerked up. "I could ask you the same question."

He shrugged. "I have work to do. I was out of the office all week."

"Me too." *Because of you.* Her unspoken comment hung in the air between them.

"I didn't realize what a hardship I was putting on you by requesting that you work with me. I'll handle it from here on out by myself."

Macie shook her head. "No, we made a bargain. I have someone starting Monday who will help me out."

Landon kept his voice businesslike. "Great. Sometimes I don't think, and I make mistakes."

Shadows filled her eyes. Was she thinking of their past relationship? He hoped that wasn't the case.

Macie's work was top quality, as it had been when they'd worked together before. He'd quickly learned they still made a good team. Well-respected, she'd made it easy for him to make inroads into learning the beat of the Saipan Hospital. He wasn't surprised she had achieved such a position of responsibility here.

He stepped into her office. "You need to go home. Take some time off. Everyone needs that."

"Like you?" Macie tapped a pen against the desk. "And aren't you the pot calling the kettle black?"

"At least I'm doing some of it outside this place."

She shrugged. "This can only be done here. I'm almost finished."

"I'll let you get back to work then. See you later." He went to his office and closed the door.

Much later, he gathered what he needed to take home. By the time he left, Macie was no longer in her office. He was glad she had gone home. But then, as he left the hospital, he glanced through the ER department door and saw Macie standing beside the nurses' desk talking to one of the staff. Clearly, Macie was still working. She seemed determined not to take his advice.

The next week followed much as the one before had as he and Macie continued to work together. Monday and

Tuesday they spent in the surgical ward, Wednesday and Thursday with the children, and Friday they worked on the cancer wing.

He'd quickly learned he missed working with patients. He'd gone into medicine because he liked helping people but also because it was a means to help provide for his mother along with Adam, his younger brother and Nancy, his sister. After his parents' horrible divorce, both he and his mother had had to work in order to pay the bills. When he joined the military out of high school his check had continued to help. As the years went by even while the navy sent him to medical school, he continued to send money home. It had been even more necessary when his mother started drinking heavily and became ill. Even his current job he had taken out of financial need after he'd left the navy. He'd had to give up clinical work to look after his family. It had only been in last few years that his help had no longer been needed. The last week had confirmed how much he loved working with patients and how much he missed it. Still, by Friday evening he was ready to get out of the building.

Tatiana had already left for the day when he stopped by Macie's office. He stood in her doorway. "I'm hungry and I know you must be too. Come on. You pick the restaurant and I'll buy."

"I have to admit that those couple of crackers and the soda I had earlier are long gone." She sounded as tired as he felt.

Landon nodded his head toward the exit. "Then let's get some dinner."

She gave him a hesitant look as if she were considering turning him down.

He stepped inside her office. "I tell you what, we'll

make it a working meal. We can talk about some of the needs we've seen over the last few days."

"Okay," Macie agreed.

For some reason he didn't like the fact that she wouldn't eat with him unless it had to do with work.

He wanted her to have dinner with him because he'd asked her.

CHAPTER THREE

A QUARTER OF an hour later, Landon walked beside Macie into the parking lot. "By the way, we're taking my car."

Macie grinned. "I rather enjoyed watching you squeezing into mine. Seeing your legs touching your nose had its satisfaction."

"So, you were laughing at me?"

She lifted her shoulder and dropped it. "Well, maybe just a little bit."

Landon didn't miss the twinkle in her eyes. He rather liked the idea that he'd put it there, even at the expense of his knees.

He was ready to drive out of the parking lot when Macie said, "Turn left. We're going to the next small town."

"I didn't know there was one."

"*Village* is a more accurate description. It's a family-owned place. It might not look like much, but the food is excellent."

"I'll trust your judgment on that."

He wasn't as sure ten minutes later when he drove the car into a gravel lot beside a building that was little more than a shack.

Inside, they sat at a small wooden table. As it was still early for dinner, very few people were there, which gave them some privacy. An older heavyset woman with an unfriendly look came to take their drink orders and then strolled back to the kitchen area.

He leaned back in his chair, leveling a look at Macie. "For a moment there I thought you were going to turn down my invitation to dinner."

"I gave it serious thought." She fingered her fork.

"Macie, I know you're angry with me over the way I left you in Hawaii, but I'd like us to at least try to be friends. I can explain what happened. I know it won't make it any better, but I had a good reason. I am sorry you got hurt. That wasn't my intention."

She studied him. Long enough that he started to squirm. "I can't imagine you having a good enough explanation that'll make up for what you did, but I would sure as hell like to hear it."

Her words were tight and sharp. He had hurt her deeply, far more deeply than he had realized. They'd had a good time back then, but he had no idea she had held on to it for this long. Could it be that he hadn't wanted to know? Because he had no intention of making it permanent, no matter how good they were together? He wasn't planning on doing that with anyone. His parents' marriage—or lack of one—had shaped his life, and he wouldn't willingly enter into that stranglehold. Love meant pain, and he'd had enough of that.

Still, maybe he should have done more to find Macie when he'd returned to Hawaii. "There was a family emergency."

She huffed and raised her hands. "That's the best you've got?"

It wasn't, but he didn't want to go into the details. That would lead to talking about stuff he really wanted to avoid...like how his father had left his family for another woman, his mother had drunk herself into financial ruin and poor health, and how Landon had been left to take care of his young brother and sister. Nope, he wasn't going to say all that. "Yes."

"Thanks for nothing. I think we're back to where we were when we came in here."

"Every time I say something you act as if you're second-guessing it. You can trust me."

Macie studied him again. She picked up a paper napkin and twisted it. "Let's just say that, based on history, I need to be careful. How do I know there won't be another—" she made air quotes with her fingers above her shoulders "—'family emergency.' Let's keep it business, Dr. Cochran. That way neither of us will expect anything and neither of us will be disappointed."

Landon winced. Something about how she said it made him think he might not have been the only person to disappoint her. He hated that he'd helped make her so cynical about people. Or was it just men?

The waitress returned with their drinks and took their order. With a scowl on her face, she nodded and walked away.

"Does she ever smile?" Landon asked in a stage whisper.

"Only when she's had too much to drink," Macie announced without lowering her voice.

Landon continued to study the menu even though he had already ordered. "Does every meal come with rice?"

"I'm afraid so. You know, we're closer to China than we are to mainland America, even though we're an American territory. All our supplies come in by boat, and I guess rice travels well."

"I guess so." He paused. "I have to admit that when I accepted your challenge to work with you, I didn't think it would be such a big deal. But it has been harder than I anticipated. I've really enjoyed being in the trenches again."

"What made you stop?"

She made it sound like he'd defected. It had been his best decision at the time. He leaned back in his chair, trying to appear more at ease than he felt. "After I was discharged from the navy, the World Health Organization made me an offer. The money was good and that was important at the time. I found I liked helping improve hospitals. Now I have a chance to head the entire organization. If I can make strides here, the job should be mine."

Her color paled for a second. "I see."

He shifted in his chair. Macie made it sound as if she might see more than he wanted her to. "Sometimes things happen in life that make us take a different path than we originally planned."

She looked up to meet his gaze. "Well, I have to admit that you're still good with a patient. Actually, one of the best I've ever seen."

Landon nodded. "Thank you. I consider that high praise."

Macie's smile sobered. Had she become uncomfortable with the direction of their conversation?

She crossed her arms over her chest. Her eyes turned thoughtful. "You said we were going to discuss your ideas for the hospital. What do you have in mind?"

Apparently, she *was* ready for a subject change. "First, let's talk about what we've learned over the last week or so."

"I can't say that I've really learned anything." She gave him a sweet smile that didn't reach her eyes.

"Okay, then I'll talk about what I've learned." He cleared his throat. "The hospital staff is a caring group. They really want to help the patients."

Macie nodded. "I couldn't agree with you more."

"But…"

Macie's brow rose.

"They're overworked," he finished.

"I agree."

"The problem areas that stand out are the lack of up-dated equipment, like a portable X-ray machine, but we both already know that. I'd also like to see an MRI ma-chine installed. Electronic charting is a must."

"That sounds wonderful to me." Excitement filled her words. "But still not new news."

"There's a lack of physicians. There's a lack of staff in a few other areas as well. Too many of the staff are working double shifts, which can lead to poor patient care and creates staff health issues. Lack of funding is a major problem. All that said, I know a number of hospitals that aren't running as efficiently as this one."

Macie blinked and sat forward. "That's good news. So, when and where does the white knight ride up with the bags of money?"

Landon didn't like that picture. He wasn't anyone's knight. Didn't want to be. "I think Pediatrics needs a complete overhaul. As does General Surgery. A number of areas need streamlining."

The eagerness in Macie's face disappeared. She sighed. "That all sounds fabulous to me, but the ques-tion still remains—where is the money going to come from? The economy here can't handle a raise in rate. And we need incentives just to get doctors to come here."

"My thought is to offer scholarships to locals to be-come doctors and nurses so that they will return to the island. It doesn't solve the immediate problem, but if we can show that there's a plan for the future, then there might be more help for the here and now."

This time excitement clearly showed in Macie's eyes. "That's a wonderful idea. Maybe you do wear white armor after all. That's an innovative way of thinking. One that I can get behind."

Maybe the white knight thing wasn't so bad. He rather liked the notion that Macie found him and his idea brilliant. It shouldn't matter as much as it did. Could it be because he had disappointed her all those years ago?

"It would not only help the hospital but the island as a whole. The hospital is one of the largest employers."

Landon held up a hand. "Don't get too excited. There'll be large hurdles to get over. It's just an idea."

"But it's a good one," she insisted.

"Apparently, you didn't think I could have one."

She crossed her arms on the table and leaned forward. "What I thought was you'd want to cut a department, fire people."

"You don't have too high an opinion of me." That knowledge hurt.

She grinned. "Would it help to know that it's improving?"

"It would." He wanted to thump his chest.

Thankfully, their waitress returned with their meals in no better humor. They ate in silence for a few minutes before Landon said, "How about telling me a little bit about this island? I've not even had a chance to see it." For some reason he wanted to know about the place she seemed to love so much.

"Would you like me to show you around tomorrow?"

The shock on her face caused him to chuckle. She hadn't planned to ask that. He purposely made a show of answering her. The look of distress on her face—and could it also be anticipation?—intrigued him. "Well, that would be nice. I'd appreciate it."

She straightened. That determination he'd seen while working with her returned. "I'll pick you up tomorrow around ten."

Macie would be keeping it strictly business if she could. "No. I'll pick you up. My car is bigger, remember?"

Macie had no idea what had possessed her to ask Landon if he wanted her to show him around. The moment the words were out of her mouth she questioned her sanity. Maybe it was that she knew how hard he'd worked the last week and a half or that there was no one else to do it. After all, she was the only person he really knew on the island. Or it could have been that she just liked him and wanted to spend more time with him. Either way, she had to honor her offer.

Against her better judgment she had slowly moved into an area where she didn't want to go. One where she became more familiar with Landon. Learning to like him, appreciate his skills as a doctor and as an administrator. Heaven help her, she was attracted to him. She didn't need any more disappointments in her life. He'd done it before. Her father had done it. What if it happened again? Could she protect herself against it?

She was ready and waiting when Landon arrived the next morning. The day before she'd given him some brief directions for finding her place. Somehow letting Landon know where she lived felt like he was invading her personal space. She couldn't complain since she was the one who had offered to show him around. Maybe he wouldn't be that interested in the island and she'd be with him for only an hour or so… She didn't think that would be the case, from what she knew about him. He'd shown an interest in every detail of the hospital. She'd be surprised if that wasn't the same regarding the island.

The second she saw Landon's car pull up in front of her place she went out to greet him.

"You do know I would've come to the door." He sounded put out.

"It wasn't necessary." She climbed into the car.

"I guess you're ready to go."

"Head along the coast road toward the hospital. We're going north."

"So tell me about Saipan," Landon said as he drove by the hospital.

"You know you can get all that from the internet." She studied him. Landon really was a good-looking man. His hair made her want to run her fingers through it. Even as he drove, his strong jaw reflected what she knew about his personality—solid, dependable and interesting. There were small creases around his eyes that implied he smiled often.

"I can, but I'm interested in hearing it from you. You've been here long enough to know what isn't in the official guide books."

"All right, I'll tell you what I know. This island was ruled by Germany until after World War One when it was turned over to Japan. During the Second World War it was stategic because of the airstrip. When the Americans arrived, there was a battle. Close to where the hospital is now is where the troops first came onshore. You can still see equipment that was left."

"Really?"

"Yep. There are small one-man tanks here and there out in the water. In one of the parks is a cement gun emplacement. In fact, they're all over the place. You just have to know what you're looking at. I'll point out one on our way to the other end of the island. Up near the airport is a large cement armory area where the headquarters were after the Americans took the island. Do you really want all this history?"

He glanced at her and smiled. "Sure, I do. I think it's interesting. Don't you?"

"I do. I like history. Okay. I'm going to leave the war for a little while. I'll tell you more when we get to where we're going."

They headed out of the well-populated area along the coast. The road rose above the ocean as they traveled. When it ended, Landon pulled into a small parking lot. "What're we going to see here?"

"From here we get a great view of the ocean and the waves washing against the rocks."

They walked over to the edge and looked down. The waves beat against the wall of stone, throwing water up at them.

When she stepped closer, Landon grabbed her arm and brought her back against his chest. Macie glanced over her shoulder at him.

"I don't want you to go over. It would look bad for me to lose my tour guide."

She liked being against his warm, strong body. There was safety and security there. Something she'd not had in a long, long time. Yet she'd been fooled before by that feeling. She'd once felt it strongly under her father's care and had come to find out that it was just an illusion; nothing had been real. She stayed a moment longer then stepped away. "When I come here it always makes me feel small. It reminds me of how little my problems are in the big scheme of things."

"That's an intriguing statement. Care to elaborate?"

"Not really." The past wasn't something she wished to revisit. She had moved beyond that time and rebuilt her life on firm ground, something real.

A few minutes later they walked back to the car.

Landon looked over the hood at her as they were getting in. "Macie, why are you out here?"

"Out here?"

His gaze met hers. "Yeah. On Saipan. So far from home."

She didn't want to get into that. No matter how much she thought she'd left what her father had done behind the old insecurity still lingered. "Because this is where I'm needed."

"Surely you could be needed closer to malls, nightclubs, friends and family." He got into the car.

She followed suit. "I've been happy here."

"Still, when was the last time you were on the mainland?" He backed out of the parking lot and headed down the road they had come in on.

Looking out the window, she said softly, "Seven and a half years."

"That long! Don't you miss civilization?"

For her, life had been made of cotton candy that had swirled down to a glob on a stick. Saipan had given her stability. She felt him watching her. "I have everything I want here, and this is where I'm needed."

Finally, he concentrated on his driving. She breathed a sigh of relief. The air had taken on that uncertain feel between them once more. Macie watched the ocean for a few minutes. Usually, she found it soothing, but for some reason it wasn't anymore. Macie didn't like the tension between them. She'd grown to appreciate their camaraderie. It would be nice to have that back.

Landon broke the silence as they headed toward town again. "Tell me about all these abandoned buildings. The ones overgrown with vines. They're everywhere."

Thank goodness he said something, Macie thought.

"About twenty years ago there was a lot of manufacturing being done here. Then the laws were changed and we started allowing manufacturing to be done outside the US where it was cheaper, and most of it went to China. Sadly, Saipan's economy suffered. Buildings were just left behind."

"Like the hotel building at the airport?"

"Yes. That's a prime example. The island was positioning itself as a tourist spot. It still is but not at the rate it once was. It was cheaper to leave it as is than to tear it down. Look down there." She pointed to a long three-story building that had obviously been a nice hotel at one time. "That was a resort. Now it's just part of the jungle."

"That's sad."

"It is. On the other side of town, we'll pass a place that looks much the same but was a shopping center. I guess the only thing visiting now are snakes and bugs. We get most of our supplies from China now. We have to place orders for the hospital at least a month ahead. I wish Washington could do more to help build industry here, but these people are resistant."

The road now ran parallel with the beach. Landon looked at the waves brushing the shore. "A lot of people seem to live the same way here, in small homes built out of cinder block. And they have chickens."

Macie chuckled. "There are a lot of chickens. I'd have a few if I had a place to house them."

"What do you like the most about island life?" Landon sounded as if he really wanted to know instead of just making conversation.

She didn't have to think about it. "The people. They're friendly and open. I also like the dress code—none of that fancy overdressed stuff is necessary."

"I can see the appeal." He patted his cargo shorts.

Landon had lightened up on his dress. Today he wore a T-shirt and khaki shorts with sandals, and he was just as impressive in those as he was in his suit. He had an air of authority about him no matter what he wore.

"You said something about tourism. Are tourists coming from the mainland?"

"Oh, no. Fifty percent of the population at any time is made up of Chinese, Japanese and Korean visitors. The other half is locals. You and I are the ones who stand out."

Landon chuckled. "I have noticed that I'm not as tan as some and much taller."

"I think you would stand out wherever you were." That slipped out before she realized she had said it.

A sexy grin covered his mouth as he looked at her. "You think so?"

She did, but she wouldn't flatter him more by answering.

His attention returned to the road. "Not going to answer, huh? Then how about this. Why don't we stop and eat somewhere before we continue the tour?"

Macie was happy with that idea since right now she just needed to get out of this small enclosed space and put some distance between them. "Okay. There's a resort down here on the left. They have a nice buffet with a Western food bar so you can get more than rice there."

"Now, that sounds nice." Happy anticipation filled his voice.

She looked at the road ahead. "I figured by now you'd want something that didn't include rice."

"You know me so well."

"Not really." She glanced at him, not missing the slight tightening of his jaw. "I have to admit, I had to get used to having rice all the time. Now I would miss it if I didn't have it. The next entrance on the left is the one you want."

* * *

Landon followed Macie to a table next to a picture window where they could look out over a lawn to the ocean beyond. They were in a large room with numerous buffet lines featuring all types of food. He'd gone for a burger and fries while Macie had chosen baked chicken, rice and a salad.

She placed her tray on the table and looked at his plate. "No rice for you, I see."

"No, I'm going for beef today. As a good Midwesterner it's required that we have it at least once a week."

Macie laughed and settled across from him. He liked the sound of her laugh. *She should do it more often*, he thought. Macie was far too serious.

They passed the time while eating talking about what they had seen that morning.

Landon had almost finished with his meal when Macie asked, "Have you ever thought about going back into practice? Start seeing patients again?"

He looked at her over his glass. "Macie, why are you pushing so hard for me to change jobs? I'm good at the one I have. If I don't do it, someone else will."

She didn't say anything for a moment. "I guess it's better having the devil you know."

His eyes narrowed. "I don't like that you think of me as the devil."

"I don't really think of you as the devil. More as an inconvenience."

"Ouch. I'm not sure that's much better." He met her look. "I'm here to help. Really."

Macie didn't appear convinced. "I'm ready to go when you are."

Soon, they were heading down the road again.

"Where to now?" Landon asked.

"We're on our way to another World War II site." She pointed out in the water. "Look there. That's one of those small one-man tanks. You can see about half of it when the tide is out."

"Why didn't they remove them?"

"I guess it was just easier to leave them. And they're a reminder of the island's history. That time was sad—I can only imagine the helplessness the locals felt."

"It was an awful time for the world in general, and to come to this small outlying island..."

"Saipan wasn't the only one affected. The tiny island just south of this one is Tinian. It's where the planes that carried the atomic bombs took off from. For a time, it was the busiest airport in the world." She chuckled. "It's even smaller than Saipan."

"Does anyone live over there?"

"They do. There's a resort that's popular as well. You have to take a single-engine plane to get there." She'd been only once.

"Sounds like an adventure."

She grinned. "The flight alone is an experience. This next place we're going is a particularly sad one."

"Sad?" He glanced at her.

"Yeah. I have a hard time thinking about it, but it's part of the island's history. You need to go at least once."

"Every place and everyone has a sad history." He knew that better than most. His mother and father had given him that. "What's this place about?"

"We're going to Suicide Cliff."

"I've heard of it. It's where the mothers threw their children off the cliff because they were afraid of what the Americans would do to them. They believed the Japanese propaganda."

"That's right. There's a small park there with a remembrance plaque telling the story of what happened." Macie pointed. "Turn up here to the right."

The road twisted up the hill and ended in a parking lot, and Landon pulled in to a spot. They walked the winding paved path beneath trees to the top of the ridge. There they stood behind a rock wall looking at the jagged cliffs below and the waves slapping against the rocky coastline.

Macie spoke as if to herself. "The beauty of the scenery is in direct opposition to the horrors that happened here. No matter how many paper fliers the Americans dropped telling the people they would not be hurt, they didn't believe it. Even the navy fired rounds against the cliff trying to get the mothers to stop. They wouldn't. They were so afraid for the future of their children they would rather have them die at their hands than chance what they had been told was coming. A mother's love, even misguided, can be astounding. Can you imagine a mother fearing for their child's future so much she'd be willing to do that?"

"I can't imagine a mother caring that much," Landon murmured.

She studied him. "That's dark."

There was an underlying question in her remark. One he didn't wish to answer. But he had opened the door and now he had to deal with the consequences. "My mother didn't care about anyone but herself. That's not true. She loved my father so much she smothered him to the point he left us all." Landon took long strides down the path in the direction of the parking lot. He didn't want to answer the question he knew Macie would have after those statements.

Macie caught up with him. "Would you like to talk about it? It might help."

And there was Macie's soft heart. Where someone else

might not want to hear his story, Macie would listen. He liked that about her. For some reason he couldn't name, he realized he wanted her to know about his family. He wanted to give her a chance to understand him. A chance to forgive him for leaving like he did.

"I can't remember a time that my mom and dad didn't fight. Loud and long. They split up when I was a junior in high school after my father found someone else. My mother started drinking. I have a younger brother and sister, who I pretty much had to raise because Mom was out of it most of the time. She started having trouble getting to work on time, then she started losing jobs. More than once we came home to find her passed out on the couch. Dad was no help. He had pretty much washed his hands of us and moved on."

"I'm sorry."

He shrugged. "Yeah, so am I. Anyway, I had good grades. I had always dreamed of being a doctor. I worked and went to the community college until my brother and sister were old enough to take care of themselves. I joined the navy with the promise of help to go to medical school. I sent all the money I could home to my family. But I still felt guilty about leaving my siblings in the situation they were in."

"You were doing what you could to make it better," Macie said softly.

He couldn't look at her. "Maybe so, but I still wasn't there for the day in, day out. We managed to convince Mom to get some help, and things did get better. My brother and sister have good brains and got scholarships to school. It took us all longer than most to get our education, but we all did it. They're both married and have babies."

Macie took his hand. "You should be proud."

He slowed his pace. "I am. My job with the World Health Organization helped make it possible."

"But what about you? You've never married and you don't have any children. Don't you want what your siblings have?"

"No."

She missed a step for a second and tugged on his hand before she rejoined his pace.

"Why not?"

"Because I grew up in the middle of an ugly marriage and saw what professing to be in love can do to someone. I never want to put another person through that or be on the receiving end of it either."

"But you would know what not to do." There was a note of earnestness in her voice.

"Maybe so, but I'm not sure I know what that kind of love really is. I certainly haven't seen it firsthand."

Macie didn't say anything more for a few minutes, but then she asked, "How is your mother now?"

Landon's chest tightened. "She passed away years ago. She developed liver cancer and only lasted six weeks after the diagnosis. I found out the morning after we spent the night together."

Macie's hiss of awareness circled around them. She let go of his hand and went still.

"I was on a plane twenty-four hours later. I wasn't thinking straight and when I returned, you were gone. I tried to find out where you were. I even asked personnel. But nothing. I'm sorry I hurt you. I never intended to. I liked you. Still do."

Macie met his look. "I'm sorry about your mother. And I'm sorry I haven't been fair to you."

"You didn't know. How could you? I wouldn't have

liked me either if I had left you like that. What I'd like to know now… Is it possible for us to be friends again?"

Macie studied him for long enough that he feared she might say no. "Yes, we can be friends."

Landon let out the breath he had been holding. He took her hand again and Macie tangled her fingers in his. It wasn't a sexual touch but one of reassurance, concern. Her eyes held shadows of pity and he didn't want that. "I didn't mean to dump all that garbage on you. I just wanted you to know why I left like I did."

"Sometimes it's just good to get it out." She squeezed his hand. "I'm glad you explained."

They continued like that as they walked to the car. Somehow, having Macie beside him eased his bitterness. His admission had changed something between them. The electricity was still there but now it was more like a steady stream instead of a spark. As if his confession had created a bond between them. The idea appealed to him.

As Landon drove back into town, he asked her, "So what do you do for fun?"

"I don't know. Read, go to the movies, swim to Bird Island, get together with friends. You know, the usual. Take a left up here."

He did as she directed. They started up a hill.

"We're on our way up Capitol Hill, the capital of the island—hence the name. No tour is complete until you have seen a capital. My parents took us to all of them in every state we visited." She paused and said quietly, "I've not thought of that in a long time."

Landon glanced at her. "Is that so?"

"Pull over here. We need to get out. We're high enough for you to see the area."

He parked, they climbed out and went to the front of the car.

"That is Tainan over there." She pointed off in one direction. "There's the hospital down there. You can see the port as well."

They stood there a few moments in silence.

"The white building behind us is the Municipal Building. It was built after the war by the US Army to use as a headquarters, and they gave it to the island years later when they no longer needed it. I figure you've already seen your side of the island, so that concludes your tour."

Landon faced her. "Thank you for taking your day off to show me around."

She wrinkled her nose. "I'm not really off today. I agreed to fill in this evening in the ER."

"And here I am taking up your time when you could be sleeping. You should've said something."

"It's no big deal. I had a good time. I haven't visited those places in a while. It was nice to see it though fresh eyes. But I really should be getting home."

When they arrived at her place, he stepped out of the car with Macie and walked her the short distance to the door.

"Thanks again for showing me around."

"You're welcome." She looked at the ground.

"Also, thanks for listening earlier. I'm sorry about what happened in Hawaii."

"And I'm sorry I didn't give you the benefit of the doubt. Let's start over." She stuck out her hand for a shake. "Friends?"

Macie wanted friendship, but he was thinking about something more. Were her kisses as sweet as he remembered? Taking her hand, he tugged her closer then leaned in. She didn't step back. Instead, she just watched him. Encouraged, he continued until his lips found hers.

He kept the kiss easy despite his desire to pull her even

closer. Regardless of the years that had passed, Macie's lips were as luscious and plump as they ever had been. Nothing had changed. Just that small touch made him want more. The spark between them hadn't lessened— if anything, it had grown hotter. His mouth moved toward hers again.

Macie's hands came to his chest, stopping him.

Disappointment washed through him, but maybe it was for the best. He wouldn't be staying here forever, and he had no intention of making her long-term promises. Avoiding such promises assured him that neither one of them would get hurt.

Yet they were adults. They were older and wiser and she certainly seemed like a strong woman now. What if they set ground rules? Couldn't they enjoy each other while it lasted? Explore this attraction?

That idea ended the moment Macie spoke. "Let's not do this. I think it's best not to complicate things. I'll see you on Monday."

Before Landon could disagree, she had closed the door between them.

He stood there looking at the door, and somehow it seemed more like a brick wall.

And he hated that it existed.

If only he could have one more kiss…

CHAPTER FOUR

MACIE WENT TO WORK on Monday with thoughts of Landon's kiss swimming in her head. She had almost floated though the evening shift in the ER thinking about him. More than one person had asked her if she was okay.

She'd enjoyed her day with Landon...too much. Even their short kiss had been enough to excite her body and let her know that those feelings she'd had for him years ago hadn't changed. If anything, they had intensified. Just another reason she had to put some space between them, to keep their interactions business only. Her heart could so easily be hurt by him. He'd even told her clearly, in his own words, that he wasn't looking for anything lasting. But she had lived through a pretend childhood, and real and forever was what she was looking for.

Even if she wanted more, her life was on this island and his was elsewhere. Landon was just passing through. It would be like Hawaii all over again, except without the misunderstanding. She wasn't putting her heart out there again, at least not with Landon. It would be too risky; there would be too great a chance of pain, and she couldn't invite more of that into her life. There had already been enough. His effect on her was no different than it had been years ago. Even though she now understood what had happened, still she couldn't take that chance. Couldn't trust…

She could still feel his pain from when he had told her about his family and the hardships he had endured. More than that, she had been impressed with the type of young man he had been when it came to taking care of his brother and sister. She'd believed her life had been difficult, but compared to his, hers had been charmed—even though it had been financed by stolen money, which spoiled the memory of it.

Still, their kiss had been nice. Better than nice. In truth, she wanted more of it. She wanted more of Landon, of everything. But she couldn't have him. He couldn't give her what she needed, and therefore the kissing had to stop.

Regardless of her feelings one way or the other, she and Landon had to work together. The sooner he had what he had come for, the faster he would be gone. And there would be less chance of her heart being broken. With Landon gone, her life would return to normal. She had to keep things between them limited to their work at the hospital and make every effort to spend no more time with him than was necessary.

That was easier said than done since they had another three days together working on the floors, and by the time Wednesday rolled around, Macie was emotionally exhausted. More than once, Landon had caught her looking at him. A spark flickered in his eyes as his lips turned up slightly. He knew too well what he did to her. To say she had been looking forward to a few days of space between them was an understatement.

With that in mind she almost skipped into work on Thursday. All went well until Tatiana came to Macie's office door. "Landon asked me to see if you could come to his office at ten this morning."

"Landon?"

She smiled. "That's what he said to call him."

Another example of Landon working his magic. "Please tell him I'll be there. Did he want me to bring anything in particular?"

"Didn't say so." Tatiana moved to leave then turned back. "He's different than the others. I like him."

All the enthusiasm Macie had started the day with disappeared. Once again, they'd be too close for her comfort. His office was the largest in the hospital but would become tiny with the two of them closed up in it. Any time she was with Landon, the world narrowed down to just him.

"Good morning, Macie," he said as she entered. He stood and, with a well-manicured hand, indicated a chair. "Please have a seat."

She took a moment to really look at him, which she hadn't dared to do in days. Landon appeared tired. His hair was mussed; stubble covered his jawline. It made him even sexier—something she shouldn't take notice of. There were smudges under his eyes. Had he not been sleeping?

"Okay. Is this something I should be worried about?" She sank into the chair.

"Not really."

Macie studied him closer. "Have you been here since we finished rounds yesterday?"

He rolled his shoulders forward then back and stretched. "Most of the time. I too had work that wasn't getting done while we were seeing patients."

Fascinated by his movements, Macie just stared. "And the idea was to catch up on everything in one night?"

He smirked. "I did go home for a few hours."

"What's keeping you awake and at this desk now?"

His brows rose with a "you have to ask that?" look. Macie's skin heated and her mouth went dry.

Landon cleared his throat, glanced down then back at her. "I wanted to discuss my findings with you."

This wasn't going to be fun. "And those are?"

"There's a lot of great care going on here, but it's hindered by the lack of staff, equipment and modernization."

"Haven't we already discussed that?" She wasn't sure she was going to like where this would lead.

"We have, but what we haven't done is figure out what we're going to do about it." Firmness filled his voice.

She crossed her arms and legs in a defensive manner. "And have you?"

"I have a few ideas jotted down. I want to run them by you and see if you have others." He folded his arms on the desk. "But your body language suggests you are not receptive to new ideas."

Macie unfolded her arms and placed them along the arms of the chair. "Is this better?"

A grin formed on his lips. Her stomach fluttered. "Much better. Please try to keep an open mind."

"Okay." She drew the word out. "What do you have in mind?"

Landon watched her closely for a moment. She shifted in the chair under his scrutiny. "I'd like to meet with each of the department leaders. Talk to them about what we saw and didn't see. Then I'd like to hear what they would like to have in an ideal world."

She nodded. So far his idea was sound.

"Then I want to meet the leadership of the island to see where they can help, what support we can count on.

Then we'll go to the staff and share our plans and ask for suggestions."

The more he spoke, the more excited she became about the ideas. She liked his use of *we*. It wouldn't be all about what *he* wanted or thought. Landon was asking for input from top to bottom. He appeared interested and concerned about all the parties and wanted their opinions. Unlike the interims who had come shouting about how they were going to improve the hospital on their own, Landon seemed like he wanted it to be a team effort.

"Your overall plan sounds good."

He smiled. "I'm glad you approve, but I hear a note of skepticism in your voice."

"I guess it's hard for me to trust after I've been burned so many times before." In all areas of her life she was careful.

Landon leaned in farther, holding her gaze. "I won't disappoint you again. I promise."

Her heart tapped a dance. She wanted to believe him. "Good."

"After we have all the information, we'll form a plan of action that I can present to my board, which will include a bid for financial help."

Macie scooted to the edge of her seat with excitement. "You'll really do that?"

"Of course I will. It's my job to make things better."

Was he doing that for the hospital or for himself? Hadn't he said this was a stepping stone to a promotion? No matter the reason, if all went as he had mapped out, then it would be to everyone's advantage.

"What do you need from me?"

"I need you to help me figure out how to approach the community leaders." He stood and paced the room. He had delivered the statement matter-of-factly and with authority. Landon had officially become the all-business administrator. Before her was a man who had formed a plan and was confident he could carry it out. For once she felt like someone might actually bring about positive change.

No longer dressed so formally, Landon was more in sync with the community. And she liked this Landon far too much.

"Any ideas?" He turned and pierced her with a look.

"I don't know... You could always just ask them for a meeting. But it would be better to meet each one casually first. Let them get to know you some. They already know about you being here because news travels fast on the island, but if they could first see you in a social setting..." She snapped her fingers as she shot out of her seat. "I know! The hash. Most of them should be there."

"What's that?"

"It's where someone cuts a path through the jungle and people follow it." She moved her hand in a hacking motion.

His face twisted up. "Huh?"

Tatiana tapped on the door and they both turned. "Sorry to bother you, but you're needed in the ER, Macie."

"Okay." She turned back to Landon. "Pick me up on Saturday afternoon at three. I'll explain it all then. Leave anything I need to know on my desk and I'll review it. Got to go."

Landon wasn't sure what he had agreed to, but he arrived at Macie's at the assigned time on Saturday afternoon. He hadn't seen her except in passing since she'd left his office two days earlier. He'd missed her. Far more than he wanted to admit.

Most of the time he'd been confined to his office working on reports and revising his ideas. His best guess was that Macie had spent the days continuing to smooth out problems within the hospital. He'd quickly learned that she had a real talent for doing so. She was good at getting people to do what she needed.

He hadn't known what to wear to a *hash* so he'd gone with T-shirt, cargo shorts and tennis shoes, figuring that since it was a Saturday afternoon the event must be casual. He knocked on her door and when she opened it, he decided he'd made the right choice because Macie was dressed much the same way.

She wore a tight faded baby blue T-shirt that showed off her curves—ones that he had a difficult time not staring at—and that had Saipan stamped across the front. Her cut-off denim shorts showed enough leg that he had a chance to appreciate each bend and dip of her skin and she too wore sport shoes. Her hair was pulled back by a band and a ball cap sat on her head, making her look much younger than she was.

Her lips were glossy pink, as if she had applied something to them. His first instinct was to kiss her to find out, but he resisted his urge, supposing she wouldn't appreciate that. After his last attempt he needed to take things slowly. He would but he still wanted to kiss her again. If she agreed he would.

Everything about Macie called to him. Why couldn't they have some fun together while he was on the island? What could it hurt? They were both adults with natural impulses.

"Hey. Come in. I'll just be a minute. I have to finish up the cookies. I was asked to bring a dessert."

"Should I have brought something?" Landon followed her through the small living area to the even tinier kitchen, which smelled like cinnamon and sugar. He looked over Macie's shoulder at the golden-brown circles. Reaching around her, he snagged one and took a bite. "Mmm…"

"Hey! Stop that. I have to have enough."

For once her voice held a playful note. Maybe them having some space from each other for a few days had been a good thing. He couldn't believe how glad he was to see her. Unable to help himself, he brought his nose close to her neck. "You smell like a cookie. Really sweet."

She straightened causing his lips to touch skin. The tip of his tongue darted out.

Macie hissed.

He stepped away, not wanting to put her on the defensive. "What can I do to help?"

"There are some uh…"

Self-satisfaction washed through him. Macie wasn't as immune to him as she wanted to act.

She cleared her throat and started again, this time sounding more in control. "I have to get these in a container. While I'm doing that, you can put the blanket and the backpack in the car."

"Consider it done." By the time he'd returned, she had a plastic container filled with cookies in her hand and was headed toward the door.

"I'm ready." She pulled the door closed behind her.

They were in the car when he asked, "Which way?"

"Back the way you came. We're going out past your place." She balanced the cookies on her lap.

"Will do. How about telling me what we're going to?" He backed out of the drive.

"Someone—or most times more than one person—cuts a path through the jungle. The rest of us follow, trying to catch them. It's a bit like a fox-and-hounds game.

The fox is the person doing the cutting and the hounds are those coming behind. Some people run while others just walk. The idea is to enjoy being out with friends. More times than not we end up at the beach where there's a big bonfire and food. A hash happens almost every weekend somewhere on the island. This particular one is being hosted by one of the mayors, so the people we want to talk to should be there."

"Good timing." He winked at her.

She grinned and nodded. "Yep."

He shouldn't be flirting with Macie. She'd made it clear where she wanted their relationship to remain, but their kiss had said something different. There was an electric attraction he couldn't resist exploring—for the short-term.

He wasn't ever going to offer her a happily-ever-after. Hell, he didn't even know what that was. He'd certainly not seen it in his parents' marriage. Their relationship left nothing but death and destruction—not something he wanted to bring into his life by choice. A relationship would never work between him and Macie anyway. She seemed planted here, while he was after a job in Washington, DC. A long-distance relationship would be an understatement in their case. Impossible.

"So what happens when you catch up with the fox, as it were? Tie them up?"

Macie giggled. He liked the sound. It was like a warm drink on a cold day.

"No, nothing like that. We don't even touch them and call 'it.'" She poked his upper arm.

"I have to say, this hash thing sounds like fun."

"If nothing else, it's unique." There was a note of pride in her voice.

He made a right turn. "I'll give you that."

They had passed his place when Macie said, "Take the next right and park wherever you can."

Landon did as he was told turning into an obviously recently cleared area creating a makeshift parking lot. They bumped over the uneven ground until he pulled next to another car and stopped. Other vehicles continued to enter the area.

"Okay. We get out and walk from here," Macie announced as she climbed out of the car. "We'll need the backpack and blanket."

"Got them." He slung the backpack strap over one shoulder and put the blanket under his arm.

Macie, with the cookies in hand, said, "This way."

The path into the jungle foliage was obvious. As they entered, the sunlight dimmed but enough remained for them to see. People overtook them as they walked but none seemed in a hurry. As they went by, many of them greeted Macie.

"If you do this all the time, why don't I see paths everywhere?"

She carefully balanced the cookies in her hands. "The vines grow so fast this path will be covered in weeks."

Macie tripped. Landon grabbed her arm to steady her. He liked touching her. Liked knowing that despite how together she acted, sometimes she needed help. "Can't we put these cookies in the backpack? At least you'd have your arms free to catch yourself if you fall."

She gave him an unsure look. "I don't want them to get crushed."

"So you'd rather fall on your face?" He looked at her with disbelief.

Macie glared at him.

Landon rolled his eyes toward the sky. "Oh, I get it. It's kind of like wearing high heels because they look good instead of your feet feeling good. You'll suffer in order to ensure your cookies arrive in perfect condition."

Macie pinned him with a look. "And you have all this wisdom about high heels from experience?"

He pulled a face and shook his head. "Heavens no. What I am is a student of human nature."

"Gotcha. As much as I hate to admit it, you might be right."

Landon took the bag off his shoulder and placed it on the ground. "Give those to me."

With obvious reluctance, Macie handed over the container of cookies. "They'd better not be in crumbs when we get to the beach."

"I promise to carry them like a baby." He wrapped the cookies in the blanket and carefully secured them in the backpack.

"I won't even ask what you know about carrying babies." She made a careful step over the rough terrain then looked at him.

He huffed. "I have handled babies before. Even delivered a few."

"I assume, with your stance on marriage, that you've never thought about having any babies of your own."

Landon wasn't sure if Macie was just making conversation or fishing for information about him. Either way, it made him nervous, as if his answer held some kind of importance to her. "I've already told you that my parents set a poor example, but living by a military schedule and then having a job where I travel all the time doesn't help when a woman wants commitment. I'm not long-term relationship material anyway."

Macie watched him as if she expected him to say more.

If he told the truth, he wasn't sure he'd be good husband or father material. It was best to stay away from the idea entirely. Plus, he'd never been with a woman long enough to take that kind of chance on her.

Her eyes narrowed. "Then you really are a 'love them and leave them guy'?"

"That's not what happened in Hawaii. I explained that."

"Got it." She started off again.

Landon pulled the backpack on. He didn't appreciate her tone of voice. It implied she didn't think much of how he handled his personal life. He caught up with her and they continued to walk in silence.

After a distance, they came to the edge of a ridge. Landon stopped. Before him lay the breadth of the island, luscious, green and humanless as far as he could see. The blue green of the Pacific met the white ribbon of sand that lined the coast. An occasional bird, a dark curve of wings, flew far below him. The handful of white fluffy clouds in the sky only added to the magnitude.

Macie hiked a few paces beyond him. She looked back. "What's wrong?"

"How can you see this view and not stop and admire it? It's amazing."

She backtracked and joined him, standing by his side.

"When I look at this, I understand why you love living here," he said as much to himself as to her. "I feel like we're the only two people in the world."

"It's beautiful. Makes me feel like my problems are small."

He glanced at her. What problems could she possibly have? "This is almost as nice as the view from my porch. It's gorgeous as well. It's my favorite spot. I love the view."

"I agree. I've had a chance to enjoy it a couple of

times when I've been to the house for a party," Macie said softly.

Landon continued looking off into the distance. "You're welcome to come by anytime. I'm more than happy to share."

"You know, Dr. Cochran, I think you might be a bit of a romantic."

He wasn't sure if that was a compliment or not. "Because I can appreciate an amazing view?"

Macie considered him for a moment, as if she had discovered something important about him. "Many people don't take the time to do even that."

Her eyes had turned warm. The temptation to kiss her almost overcame him.

Thankfully, she stepped away. "We'd better get going so we're at the beach before dark. I can assure you we don't want to be on the path after the sun goes down." She started off.

They were now going down a slope. The walking became much more difficult, but they remained side by side.

"What's the plan to get us back to the car?" He hoped it wasn't wandering through the jungle again.

"We'll catch a ride with somebody to the car park." She reached for his arm as she took a step down then quickly released it.

A small group overtook them and one of the men said, "Hi, Macie. I'm glad to see you could make it."

"Hey, Luc. It's good to see you. Thanks for the invitation. Hashes are always good exercise."

The rest of the group moved on ahead of them and waited while Luc spoke to him and Macie. "That they are." The man glanced at Landon.

Macie put her hand on Landon's bicep briefly. "Luc, this is Dr. Landon Cochran. He's the interim administrator for the hospital. I brought him along. I thought I'd give him a real taste of island life."

The local man of medium height, thick shoulders and brown skin chuckled, "A hash will do that."

Landon took the opening Macie offered and extended his hand. "Nice to meet you, Luc."

Luc gave Landon a toothy grin. "You too."

"I'm interested to see what this—" Landon waved his arms "—is all about."

"The best is yet to come. I promise. In fact, I need to get going if I'm going to oversee things." He waved and rejoined his group.

When the man was out of sight Macie said, "He's the mayor of one of the larger villages. One we should talk to."

"He didn't give us much chance to talk business," Landon commented.

"Right now isn't when you want to do that. We'll call for an appointment later. After meeting you tonight they can put a face to the name. They'll remember you and give you some time."

"I see."

They continued around a large boulder that they had to hold on to. Soon, they were out of the foliage, then they had to climb down over rock to reach the sand. Closer to the water a bonfire burned and people stood in clusters around it. Off to one side a couple of long tables had been set up. Food filled both of them.

Landon followed Macie as she made her way toward the tables. Once again, a number of people called out her name then waved. He'd never in his adult life stayed in one place long enough to build those types of relationships. What would it be like to have friendships like that?

"I hope my cookies made it," Macie murmured.

He did too. If he weren't larger than Macie, he might have feared for his life. At the table he lowered the pack and unzipped it. Gently, he removed the blanket then the container and handed the cookies to her.

Macie opened it carefully. With a proud lift of her chin, she placed the cookies on the table with the other desserts.

Landon breathed a sigh of relief. All the cookies had arrived intact, and she beamed up at him. A ripple of warmth washed through him, making him feel like a hero. He grinned. Macie was anxious where her cookies were concerned. He leaned in close and whispered for her ears only, "I'm sure everyone will love them."

Even in the darkening light he could see her blush. She smiled and his heart almost jumped out of his chest.

"Stop teasing me and let's find a place to sit." She started toward the fire.

They found a spot among the other blankets and Landon spread theirs out. Macie took the backpack from him, sat it on the blanket and started removing items they would need to dine. One she was done, she looked around.

"Now, let's go see and be seen."

Over the next half hour she introduced him to a number of the guests. A few were influential people from the villages, including another mayor. Landon was careful not to mention the business of the hospital, despite his first inclination to do so. He and Macie were in the middle of a discussion that included a great deal of laughter when Luc, the man they had met on the path, called for everyone's attention.

"Welcome. Thanks for joining us. We hope you enjoyed the trail down today. Now help yourself to something to eat and stay as long as you wish."

Landon tugged her hand. "Let's go get some of that food. I'm hungry after that walk, and I'm eager to try another one of your cookies."

Macie said over her shoulder, "I hope you aren't disappointed."

They stopped by the blanket and picked up their plates.

"I'm not sure I could ever be disappointed in anything you do."

Her brows drew together with doubt. "I think you might be trying too hard to flatter me. It's not necessary."

"I'd never say what I don't mean."

She smirked at him. "People do it all the time."

Landon wondered who had hidden something from her. Someone she really cared about? An old boyfriend? The idea of her caring about another man somehow bothered him. He held no claim on her, now or years ago. And he had no intention of doing so either.

They joined the buffet line. Famished after their trek, he didn't hesitate to pile his plate full of food. Macie was a little more subdued, but she had covered all the space on her plate as well.

He reached out his hand. "Give me your plate to hold and you can fix us a dessert plate to share. Be sure to put a couple of your cookies on it."

Macie lifted her chin and gave him a defiant look. Landon needed to learn that he couldn't order her around outside the usual chain of command in a medical situation. "Giving orders, Doctor?"

He smiled. "Merely making a suggestion."

She removed the extra plate she'd put under her other one and handed him her food. "Any other type of dessert you'd like?"

"I trust your judgment." The words were thrown over his shoulder as he walked away.

Macie filled the plate with sweets and returned to their blanket. It suddenly occurred to her that she and Landon sharing a blanket might send the wrong message. She looked at the desserts. The two of them sharing a plate of food was even worse.

Landon waited, sitting cross-legged on the blanket. He'd even gone to the open cooler and picked them up iced drinks. Reaching for the plate she held, he took it from her. She exhaled and sank to the blanket.

"What's the sigh for?"

Great. She hadn't planned to do that out loud. "Nothing."

He watched her for a second, then picked up his plate and began eating. She joined him.

"This is all delicious. I'm not sure if it's because I'm so hungry or because everyone is such a good cook." Landon forked a bit of barbequed meat.

"Probably a little bit of both. Eating outside always makes the food taste better."

It didn't take Landon long to clean his plate. He went back for more.

Macie put her plate to the side when she'd finished, and smiled when she saw Landon returning with his plate overflowing again.

"Don't wait on me to start on your dessert," he said.

She placed her hands in her lap. "I don't think I'll have any."

He studied her. "What? If I remember correctly, you used to have a sweet tooth."

He remembered her well. She thought he'd completely forgotten her after he'd left her in Hawaii. She had no idea she'd made that much of an impression on him.

"Come on. You can share, can't you? Except the cookies are all mine." He grinned as he handed her a clean fork.

"I can share." She feared he might charm her into sharing too much with him. Like a kiss, or...more.

When they finished their dessert, Landon set the plate off to the side then leaned back on a bent arm and crossed his ankles. He appeared relaxed. Even in the low light of the fire she saw him studying her. "That might have been the finest meal I've ever eaten. And your cookies are to die for."

She couldn't help but smile, tickled he liked them so much. "Now you're making fun of me."

"No, I'm not. They were great. I'm just sorry there weren't any more to be had."

"Okay, you don't have to go overboard. You can stop now."

Landon's look turned serious. "Only if you promise to make me a plate of my very own some time."

Macie raised a hand. "All right, you win."

He looked around at the other people for a moment. "Is there anyone else that I need to meet tonight?"

She shook her head, a little out of sorts with his scrutiny. "No, we did better than I expected. On Monday I'll have Tatiana start making calls for appointments."

"You know, the military could use your drive and organizational skill when they plan their missions."

She grinned, sitting a little straighter. "I'll take that as a compliment."

"It was meant that way," he said softly.

They both were quiet for a few minutes. She was enjoying the warmth of the fire, the slight breeze off the water and the fact Landon was near.

"Macie, I still don't understand why you're really in

this far-flung place." His voice was low enough that it could have been her subconscious whispering to her.

She'd not expected his question. The truth, even so many years later, was still too raw to share. "I'm making a living."

"You could be doing that anywhere. Why here? Why would a young, attractive, determined, vivacious woman, who could be enjoying parties, movies and having a love life, want to live so far away from the bright lights?"

"Who said I don't have a love life?"

He raised a brow. "Do you?"

"No."

"Why, Macie?" His voice soothed and begged at the same time.

What will it take to get him to stop pushing? "I told you how I came to work here."

"Yes, you did. But not why or what has kept you here. Don't you miss your family, friends, shopping?"

"I talk to a few friends when I can. One has come to visit for a week." She lifted her shoulders proudly. She wasn't as pitiful as he was making her out to be. But the friend who had come to visit was someone she had met in Hawaii, not a childhood friend. She hadn't kept in touch with any of those because her father had stolen from some of their parents.

He gave that a moment of thought. "Seems a long way to come for such a short visit."

"It was. I appreciated her coming. It was great to see her." The truth was she been thrilled and surprised.

"What about your family?"

He needed to stop. She didn't want to talk about the real why. Didn't want to go to that dark place. She rarely shared the true reason. More like *never* shared. But Landon had told her about his parents, his life growing up. Didn't he deserve the same consideration from her? What could it hurt? She lived halfway around the world now. Cameras and journalists would never be in her face again as long as no one knew who she was.

"Okay, since you seem to want to know so badly, then I'll give you the dirty details. I came for the reason I have already told you. I was assigned here and I've stayed here because I'm needed."

"But there's more."

She took a deep breath. It was time. "Yes. My father is Jason Beck. He was head of Limited Investments. Does that ring any bells?" Macie glared at him. She hated talking about this.

Landon sat up and turned toward her. "It sounds familiar, but I'm not sure why."

"It's because he—my family—was on TV and in newspapers for months. My father bilked people out of their money, took all their retirement savings."

"Oh, I remember now."

It sounded as if Landon had started to get it. "My father had been running a Ponzi scheme for years. He destroyed a lot of people's lives. I'd grown up living a life of luxury while my father had been busy stealing from people. I had just finished nursing school when it all exploded. To help my father, the lawyers said the family needed to stand beside him. We needed to appear as a united force, regardless of what we might have thought. I worshipped my father. I was his little princess. But everything in my life had been a lie. When the trial was over, I had to get away. Go somewhere where I wasn't recognized, so I joined the traveling nurses and ended up here."

"I understand now. But that was years ago, wasn't it? Haven't you ever wanted to go back?" His hand came to rest over hers. There was something reassuring and comforting about it.

"Occasionally, but Saipan feels like home now. I'm needed here. I'm not in the spotlight, and that suits me just fine."

Before she could say more or Landon could comment, out of the dark a voice yelled urgently, "Macie? Where are you?"

CHAPTER FIVE

LANDON'S HEAD JERKED AROUND at Macie's name.

She called back, "Over here, Joe."

A man came running toward them. Landon stood and helped Macie to rise.

"You're needed." Joe pulled in a deep breath. "There's been an accident on one of the tankers. A man has fallen through the cargo opening into the hold."

Macie set off toward Joe before he'd finished speaking. The stricken look on her face had told Landon this wasn't good and the adrenaline started pumping immediately. Landon didn't know if the call for help included him, but Macie wasn't leaving without him. He jogged after her.

Shouting off rapid-fire questions, Macie moved into a lope. She asked Joe, "You have a vehicle?"

"Yeah."

"Let's go." She joined the man, and Landon came alongside her. "Where's the ship worker?"

"He hit a container and then went down between them. Worse, it's the ship's medical man."

"Great," Macie mumbled. She didn't slow as she followed Joe. "He's alive?"

"They heard him make some noise right after he fell." Joe kept pushing their pace forward.

"They haven't tried to move him, have they?" Concern wrapped Macie's words.

"The dispatcher told them not to," Joe said.

"Good."

They soon reached parking area, and Joe indicated to a Jeep. Macie climbed in the front passenger seat and gave Landon a startled look when he jumped in behind her. Had she been so focused on what was ahead that she had forgotten about him?

"When did the call come in?" She returned to asking Joe questions.

"Fifteen minutes ago." Joe put the vehicle in gear and made a turn in the sand, slinging it in a wide arc. They quickly hit the pavement and were barreling down the road with the emergency lights flashing. "The ambulance team is out on a run. That's why I came after you. They'll get there behind us. Hopefully, only five or ten minutes."

Macie braced herself against the dashboard. "Yet every minute counts. Is a boat waiting for us at the dock?"

"Yes."

Boat? Landon hadn't thought that far. They were going to have to take a boat to the ship? It wasn't at the dock?

Joe glanced back at him with a questioning look. Macie said, "You haven't met Dr. Cochran yet, have you? He's our interim administrator."

Joe nodded. "Yeah. I heard about him." That didn't sound like a positive thing to Landon's ears. In his type of work, he wasn't always popular. For some reason, this time, he wished it were different.

"Joe's one of our EMTs. He's supposed to be off tonight too." Macie sounded accepting as if it happened often to lose her leisure time. They pulled up in a parking lot near a long, wide industrial pier. He'd previously seen it only from a distance when Macie had been giving him the tour of the island.

"Pete's waiting to take us out to the ship," Joe said as they started down the pier.

"Pete?" Landon asked.

"Yeah. Local guy we call on sometimes," Macie offered.

Waiting near the end of the pier was a speedboat. The three of them ran toward it and climbed in. Pete had the boat running, and as soon as they were seated, he took off.

The sky was inky black. The only lights were those coming from the huge tanker ahead of them.

As Macie held her hair out of her face, she leaned in close to Landon and said, "The reef won't allow the ships to come in any closer. They anchor offshore and everything must come in by smaller boats."

Moments later, Pete backed off the gas and they slowly traveled over the reef. Beyond it, he gave the boat gas again and they thumped and bumped across the wavy water to the oceangoing tanker. Macie grabbed Landon's leg to steady herself over one particularly rough dip and rise. Clouds drifted over the moon and visibility decreased.

Landon glanced back. The lights of the coast were tiny in the distance.

Not quickly enough for Landon, Pete pulled alongside the ship. A large door stood open a few feet above the waterline and a metal ladder hung down over the side. Joe reached for the ladder and started up it. Once Joe stepped inside, Macie didn't hesitate to do the same. But Landon wasn't as enthusiastic. He held out his hands in case he needed to assist her or catch her if she fell, but neither happened. When his turn arrived, he followed suit, leaving the rocking boat behind. Soon, they were all standing in a wide space that ran the width of the belly of the tanker.

Macie spoke to a man whose accent told Landon English wasn't his first language. His short stature and straight black hair showed his Asian descent. Bringing a radio to his mouth, he talked rapidly into it, and someone answered him in Chinese. The group moved farther into the center of the ship and stepped into a large freight elevator. They then exited high above where they had entered the ship, and after going down a short passage, they went through a door onto the outside deck.

Landon looked around. The lights blared and everything around them was huge, intimidating. The entire experience would be surreal if he had been allowed to dwell on where he was and what he was doing. He was out of his element. Macie seemed to take it all in stride. Apparently, she had been on one of these hulking ships before.

They continued across the floodlit riveted metal floor to a gigantic hole surrounded by rails: the cargo hold. Their party joined a group wearing hardhats, standing nearby. Macie spoke to the man with the radio, and he pointed down into the darkness in the center of the ship.

Landon had tried to imagine what Joe and Macie had been discussing on their drive, but this situation was far beyond any scenario he had pictured. In his opinion, it was past the skills of he and Macie. Yet he knew something must be done for the injured man. Hopefully, they wouldn't be too late.

"I need to get down there," Macie said.

"The only way down is by crane." The crew member indicated with a hand the large piece of equipment mounted on the deck.

"Can't we go in from the floor we were just on?" Landon asked, standing beside Macie.

The man shook his head. "No. The man is between shipping containers. This is the only way to reach him."

"Okay, then get me down there," Macie stated.

"If anyone is going in there, it's going to be me," Landon announced.

"You're not—"

Landon gave her a stern look. "We're wasting time. You can better help organize things up here. I'll assess what's needed and let you know." He asked the man, "Do you have radios that we can use?"

The man with the radio nodded then said something to another sailor. He hurried off. "We already have a couple of men down there waiting to help."

Macie remained silent so long that Landon feared she would disagree with his plan, but she finally gave him a firm nod.

"Okay," he said to the man with the radio, "send me down."

The sailor returned with the radios and handed one to each of them.

"You'll need to ride in the harness seat." The man started toward the crane and the cables dangling from it.

Landon moved to follow but a hand on his arm stopped him.

Macie gave him an earnest look. "Be careful."

He gave her a wry smile. "I will."

Not a fan of heights, all too soon Landon found himself sitting in a metal seat slowly being lowered into the center of a huge hole. Using a headlight Macie had handed him from somewhere, as well as the handheld flashlight that a crew member had shoved into his hand at the last second, he searched the area and saw two men waiting on top of a container.

It took longer than he would have wished before his feet touched a steel floor. Landon used the radio to let Macie know he had arrived. She sounded relieved. Soon, the crane operator pulled the basket up again.

"Do either of you speak English?"

"Little," one of them said.

Landon was glad to hear that. "Show me where the injured man is."

The sailor nodded and pointed down. "Watch step."

He was right—the rough and ridged surface was a tripping hazard. Landon stepped over the lip running the width of the container.

The man pointed between two stacks of oceangoing boxes.

A couple of thick ropes were coiled nearby. He and the sailors needed to be tied off so they wouldn't fall as well. Landon found an end and secured it around his waist, then looped it through a metal ring welded to the container. Secured, he went down on his belly and looked into the narrow space between the boxes.

Finally, he saw a flash. He focused the beam of light in that direction again. It was the reflective tape on the man's orange work coveralls. Landon radioed, "I see him."

"His position?" It was Macie speaking.

"About eight feet down. No movement. One leg is in an odd position. Best guess is it's broken. We need more rope. The emergency basket, neck brace, leg brace and some manpower."

"Ten-four."

Landon called down to the man. "Can you hear me? We're here to help. Hang on."

The man who spoke English lay on his stomach beside Landon, looking over the lip.

"Tell him in Chinese we are coming after him," Landon instructed.

The man nodded and spoke. Still no noise or movement from the injured man.

Landon hoped they were not too late. Until he had the medical supplies, there wasn't much more he could do. Soon, the basket was being lowered again. This time it was with Macie in it, her lap full of supplies.

Landon took the large bag from her, then helped her out of the seat. He then radioed up that the contraption could be raised.

"Where's the man?" Macie asked, starting to cross the container.

"Hook yourself up first. I can't have you going over." Landon attached the other rope to the same hook he was using and tied her off. While he worked, he told her, "Don't take any chances."

Her chin jutted out. "I won't."

"This way." Landon led the way to the side. He wouldn't have her getting hurt. For some reason he felt responsible for her.

As they looked over the edge, Macie asked, "Have you formed a plan?"

He had, but he didn't particularly like it—but then he didn't think they had a choice. "We're going to have to go down and get him. Bring him up here before getting him into the emergency basket. We'll have to pull him up here manually since there's so little space."

"Joe's on his way down, along with a few other men for man power. I'll go down to the injured man. I'm the smallest and he'll need a neck brace at minimum. There's no way he doesn't have head trauma. To make matters worse, a storm is coming. The wind is picking up. We need to get this guy out of here and to shore."

Landon didn't like the proposal, but he had to agree with her. The space was so narrow he wouldn't even get close to the man before getting stuck.

Joe arrived with more equipment and the seat went back up. Joe tied himself off with a rope he'd brought down as Macie explained the plan.

Landon hated the idea of her being the one to go down, but outside of his personal issues with it, he couldn't think of a reason to stop her.

He helped her get into a harness that the ship had provided while Joe fastened the rope. Landon then found the neck brace and gave it to her. But figuring she couldn't hold it and see about protecting herself, he took it back from her and secured it to another rope. He would lower it down to her when she was ready.

He placed his hands on her upper arms, holding her in place, and looked into her eyes. "You ready for this?"

"I don't really have a choice, do I?" She wore a resigned but determined look.

"No, not really. I'll be right here when you come up. Don't take any chances." He gave her a quick kiss on the lips and squeezed her arms. "I wouldn't want to lose you now that I have found you again. Now, let's save this man."

Macie's mouth formed a firm line before she went to her knees and then her belly. Rolling over, she slid over the side feetfirst. He and Joe slowly let out the rope holding her.

"Hold right there. I've reached him," Macie called, not using the radio.

She must be afraid she might drop it. Landon could hear his heart beating in his ears.

"He's alive. Barely. Leg is a compound fracture. Bleeding but not pouring. Head trauma."

"Can you put on the neck brace?" Landon yelled.

"No. Send me another rope. I need to secure him then have you bring him up some before I try to put on the brace."

"I've got her." Landon sat and braced his feet against the small ledge running the length of the container.

Joe grunted and hurried to the pile of supplies.

Thankfully, one of the crew took over Joe's position, easing the strain on Landon. Joe threw the line over the side.

Minutes went by and he heard nothing from Macie. He could stand it no longer. "Macie?"

"I'm working here. Almost done."

More long moments stretched out, then she called, "Pull up gently on his line."

Joe and one of the others did so.

"Okay. Now mine."

Landon pulled hand over hand, slowly bringing her up.

"Stop there. Send down the brace," Macie called.

Joe put it over the side.

"I'm getting it into place," Macie called up.

Landon felt Macie's movement through the rope.

"Macie?" he called.

"Almost have it in place."

He was ready to have her back up with him safe and sound. Was there a hand squeezing his heart? He'd never felt like this about another person before. Fear was like a real thing eating at him.

Finally, she called, "Okay. Slowly pull him up."

Again, her movements came through the rope. He couldn't stand not being able to see her. It was time to get her out.

"Stop, stop."

Landon held his breath until Macie called, "Okay, but super slow. Landon, start pulling me up as well."

Using all his strength, he pulled the rope through his hands. The muscles in his thighs quivered and those on his back ached with his effort. Time ticked by slowly.

"Hold me right here. Ease the patient up and over while I steady his legs. Watch the left one."

"Give me a second." Landon looked at the only man left who wasn't doing something and indicated with his head for him to take Landon's place. He hated to leave Macie, but he would be needed immediately to work on the injured man. He handed over the rope and stood. His legs were cramped, but he shook them out.

"Okay. I'm ready." Landon went down on his hands and knees so he could see over the side.

Macie looked up at him. All he wanted to do was haul her into his arms and make sure she was safe, but he had work to do. He gave her his best reassuring smile.

"Okay, guys, pull him up slowly." Landon reached for the patient as soon as he could grasp him and eased him up by placing his hands under his arms. Landon made every effort at gentleness. As the man's hips came over the side, Landon's focus went to seeing to the leg. He held it steady as he was brought onto the container to lie unconscious on his back.

"Get Macie up," he barked at Joe.

On the radio, he heard that the emergency staff were leaving the hospital and heading toward the pier. At least there would be more medical help coming. For now, it was him, Macie and Joe. Landon glanced over to where the men worked Macie's line. He could just now see the top of her head.

"Joe, I need an IV started STAT. The man has a head

injury as well. I've not had time to check for further injuries, but I'm starting now."

Macie had heard Landon's demand as she was being hauled up. Glad she now sat on top of the container and was out of the narrow space hanging by a rope, she took a deep breath. She'd trusted Landon to take care of her, but that didn't mean she had liked being squeezed in between two pieces of metal, unable to see the bottom—not that she'd wanted to.

To her knowledge, Landon had never encountered an emergency like this before, yet he'd been impressive in his command of the situation despite no longer regularly working on the frontline of emergency medicine.

Nursing school hadn't trained her to carry out a roped rescue. All she knew was that a man would die if she didn't do something, terrified or not. Standing, she paused a moment to gather her wits and take another deep breath to settle her pounding heart.

"We need more light here," Landon said.

The man who spoke English translated for the crew members, who then pointed their flashlights over the patient.

Landon slowly worked his fingers over the man's head. She'd seen the large gash on the patient's forehead, but in the poor lighting she'd not been able to determine if he had additional injuries.

"I'll do the vitals." Macie went to the bag and pulled out the stethoscope and blood pressure cuff.

Landon's gaze met hers. An intensity filled his eyes she'd not seen before. "Nice to have you back."

She smiled. It felt good to have someone concerned about her. It had been a long time. Since she had left her family, in fact. She'd heard Landon demand that she be taken care of, the worry in his voice evident. "Nice to be up here again."

His hands were now working their way over the patient's shoulders and down his rib cage.

"BP ninety over fifty, heart rate one ten and thready. He's lost a good deal of blood. We'll need to start plasma and plan for a blood transfusion ASAP. Where are those emergency guys?"

Just then the radio squawked. "The EMTs are at the pier, just waiting on the boat to come get them."

She reached for the radio. "Can you patch me through to them?"

"Yes."

A few seconds later she heard the voice of one of the EMTs.

"This is Macie. Stay where you are. We're coming to you. Tell the ER to have whole blood waiting. Also, call Guam and have them on standby to send the jet. This case is more than our ICU can handle."

"Ten-four" came back through the radio.

"We have a head injury, open wound. Compound break of the femur. Patient is unconscious. Eyes are…"

Landon lifted the man's eyelids. "Fixed and dilated."

She relayed the information and then gave the rest of the vitals. "We'll be on our way as soon as we have him in the basket and out of this hole. When we're on the transfer boat I'll radio again."

The patient barely clung to life. One thing at a time. They had to keep him alive long enough to have surgery and receive more intensive care.

A big fat drop of rain hit Macie's arm. She looked up. Through the deck floodlights she could see the rain falling. Now they would have to contend with the weather.

"It's starting to rain. The water will be getting rough. Let's get him in the basket and up on deck."

"Macie, you go up first and organize things. I'll come up behind the patient."

A man quickly attached the crane seat to the cables and Macie soon rose in the air on the way to the deck. On this ride she spent some time looking around. She couldn't believe she'd been inside a tanker, much less sandwiched between two metal boxes.

At the top she conferred with the lead man about using the ship's wider, flatter and slower ferryboat to get the injured man to land. Someone handed her a well-used yellow slicker, which she gratefully pulled on. The rain had picked up and the deck was slippery. She waited impatiently for the crane to lift her patient out.

When he arrived, she quickly checked his vitals and made sure he had been secured for the trip across the water. She then supervised him being carried to the elevator. On the way she glanced at the dark hole, hoping Landon would soon appear. He would have to catch up since there was no time to wait on him.

She saw to securing the patient in a boat belonging to the ship used to transport small cargo and men. It was wider and more stable than the speedboat. The captain was ready to cast off when Landon came running out the doorway. He scrambled in, flopping into the nearest seat, still in only the clothes he'd been wearing when he'd boarded the ship.

As they took off, she called, "You good?"

He did a thumbs-up.

The rain beat down on them, but the boat kept moving. She pulled off the slicker, sat in the bottom of the boat and held it over the patient's face. Looking up, she saw Landon grimacing as he braced against the rain and wind.

The flat-bottomed boat made for a bumpy and slow trip. Shivering and soaked through, she tried not to think about it. Their patient needed the attention. He wasn't at the hospital nor out of trouble yet.

By the time the boat reached the dock, the wind had increased and the rain beat down harder than ever. The bad weather had turned into a storm. Getting close enough to the cement pier without smashing into it and then not dropping the patient into the water as they got him out would be a challenge, but it must be done. They were still fighting against the clock. It had been too long since the call had first come in.

It required some maneuvering on the captain's part to bring the craft alongside the pier. Thankfully, there were enough people in the boat and waiting on the dock to lift the litter. As quickly as possible, and between swells in the water, they removed the patient without too much difficulty. With heads down against the pouring rain, they hurried to the waiting ambulance.

It was a relief to hand the patient over to the EMTs. Because there wasn't enough room in the ambulance, one of the police officers offered her and Landon a ride to the hospital. Landon put an arm around her shoulders, shielding her against the pounding rain and offering his warmth, as they hurried to the car. They piled into the back seat.

Landon huffed and scooted next to her. "To be out of the weather feels great."

She shivered. "Better than great. Do you think this guy is gonna make it?" She was in need of reassurance that all their efforts wouldn't have been for nothing.

He squeezed her hand. "I don't know, but I do know we gave it our best effort."

Far too often she'd given her best effort and still it

hadn't made a difference. Like when she had stood beside her father and he had still gone to jail. Or when she'd demanded they do something for the people he had hurt, the lawyers had just laughed at her. She'd been as helpless then as she was now. Nothing about being at other people's mercy appealed to her.

At the hospital the officer pulled his car up behind the ambulance, which now stood empty with its back doors wide open. She and Landon hurried inside the hospital and headed straight to the area where the staff huddled around their patient.

"What can I do?" Macie asked.

Landon took her elbow. When she tried to pull away, his grip tightened and he gently drew her out of the room.

"We both need dry clothes and to take a moment to regroup. Our patient is in good hands. We'll ask what we can do after we take care of ourselves."

She jerked her arm, but he tightened his grip. "But—"

"Macie, you can't be everything to everybody all the time. You have to let go sometimes."

She screwed up her face and gave him an unhappy glare. "I call the shower first."

He barked a dry laugh. "Okay. Where's the on-call room?"

"This way." She led him down the hall to a door on the right. Knocking, and not receiving a response, she entered. Hating to admit it, Macie had to allow that Landon was right. Her teeth had started to chatter; she was cold, wet and uncomfortable. Coming into an air-conditioned building hadn't helped. A shower and dry clothes would be heavenly. After she took care of herself, she'd be in a position to help again.

"If we're not careful we'll have hypothermia." Landon stepped into the bathroom and turned the shower on. Still standing in the sleeping area Macie heard the water running.

"In the tropics?" she asked.

"It can happen. In truth I was getting worried you might be in shock back there in the boat." Landon came to stand in the bathroom doorway.

She started kicking off her soggy shoes. "No. Not shock. Just exhaustion."

"And coming down off an adrenaline high. I know the feeling. I bet Joe does too. I'll check on him when he arrives."

"Now, into the shower." Landon stood out of the way and motioned for Macie to enter.

She stepped forward and by him, still wearing her clothes.

"Don't take too long or all the hot water will be gone," Landon said. "If I think that's happening, I'll join you."

Something about the determined look in his eyes made her think he meant it.

Macie swung around and glared at him. "You wouldn't dare!"

Landon's eyes narrowed, his look meeting hers. "Stay too long and just see what I do. I'm cold and miserable and more than ready to get out of these clothes. Now, get busy."

He wasn't kidding. She had better get moving. With a gulp, Macie closed the door between them. After stripping off her damp clinging clothes, she stood under the water. She sighed with pleasure. What if Landon did do as he threatened? A tingle of awareness rippled through her. She might like it. Too much.

Lifting her face to the spray, Macie couldn't help but enjoy the feel of the water flowing over her. Her thoughts went to the events of the last few hours. She'd been hanging from a rope. Everything about the experience had been dangerous. Suddenly, she doubled over sobbing. The tears poured down with the water. What was wrong with her? She never cried. Certainly not for herself. Not since her father's trial.

"Macie, honey, what's wrong? I knocked and you didn't answer."

Landon was there. He turned her in his arms and brought her against his broad bare chest, cupping her head as he held her against him. The sound of his steady heartbeat somehow comforted and excited her at the same time. Despite her tumultuous emotions following their experience that night, her blood zipped through her veins in reaction to being so close to a bare-chested Landon. He wore only his shorts.

She wrapped her arms around his waist. He felt so strong and reassuring, so right.

After a few minutes, his voice filled with concern, he asked, "Are you hurt?"

"No." The word was accompanied by a sniffle.

"Then what's going on?" She felt his compassion in his embrace yet there was also a hum of sexual consciousness between them. Landon held her gently, tenderly, but she had the sensation he was holding himself back.

She mumbled against his neck, "I was so scared."

"I know, honey. I'm glad I wasn't the only one." He kissed the top of her head.

"Mmm." Macie ran a hand over the muscles of his lower back and snuggled closer. Landon felt so good. Why couldn't she let go just once? Let Landon show her how alive she could feel.

Landon felt Macie's smile against his skin. Her hand moving over his back sent heat shooting throughout his body. He was hyperaware of every move she made. He'd stepped into the shower to comfort her and now his body ached to consume her. Between them, he had grown hard with desire. If their embrace didn't end soon he would be asking for more than she might be willing to give.

Macie looked at him with wide eyes. "You were afraid too? It didn't show."

It might not have shown, but he'd felt it all the way to his bones. He had no wish to repeat any of it, especially the part where Macie had hung by a rope.

"That doesn't mean I wasn't worried." He cupped her cheek and lowered his mouth to hers. She tasted so sweet. All he intended to do was reassure himself that she was there, safe and sound. Yet her lips were plump, damp from the water and salty from her tears. She felt like heaven. He kept the kiss gentle, comforting, despite his desire to do more and his control that had become razor thin.

It felt good to be alive. Macie made him feel that way.

She moaned, and her arms came up around his neck as her perfect velvety smooth body leaned into his.

Landon ran a hand down the length of her damp back, stopping himself just short of going too far out of bounds. This wasn't, shouldn't be, about sex but about comfort. But his body begged for the former. Regardless of the fact that he held a naked Macie—which he'd dreamed of doing every night since arriving on Saipan—he couldn't, wouldn't, take advantage of her. If the circumstances were different, would she be letting him hold her like this?

They had to stop now. This wasn't the time or the place. He wouldn't take the chance that she might resent him or regret being with him.

Stepping away from her and breaking the kiss, he

turned her and pulled the shower curtain back. With his palm on her lower back, he gave her a gentle push. "Dry off and get dressed. I put some clean scrubs on the counter."

She stepped out, and he firmly drew the curtain between them, grateful the water had cooled. It saved him from having to turn it to cold.

Macie had left by the time he came out of the bathroom. He was glad, since he had no idea what her reaction would be after she'd had time to think about those moments in the shower. Putting his feet back into his wet shoes, he headed to where he'd last seen their patient.

On arriving, he saw Macie standing at the unit desk holding the phone. "We need the plane here ASAP."

He stopped beside her. Macie glanced up then away as if she didn't want to make eye contact. Was she embarrassed by her actions in the shower? He was hoping she would want to repeat them when her mind had cleared. His body still begged for her to do so.

Macie's attention returned to the phone, "The patient has head trauma. He needs Level One trauma care. He has to come to Guam and then go on to another hospital to get it." There was a pause. "I know there's a storm. I've been out in it trying to save this man's life." Another pause. "Okay, okay, I understand. Just send it when you can." Macie dropped the phone on the hook.

"I'm guessing the plane from Guam can't make it until the storm breaks."

"Correct. The CT scan shows a swelling of the brain. All we can do right now is take him to ICU and wait until he can be flown to Guam. Even the surgery for the leg will have to wait."

"You have done all you can for tonight. He's in good hands now. It's time we go home."

"I don't want to leave until I know he's safely in ICU." Macie turned toward where the man still fought for his life.

"Okay, but the minute he's settled, we're going to get some rest." Landon gave her a firm look.

"You can go on home." A hopeful note entered her voice.

Was Macie trying to get rid of him? "Not going to happen. I too want to see him settled in ICU."

A few minutes later they helped push the patient's gurney to ICU. Landon listened to the ER doctor's report and added a couple of notes that he knew from the accident scene. While he did that, Macie stayed busy assisting the nurses as they hooked the patient to the monitors and organized the IV lines.

The patient had been settled in ICU, and finally there was nothing left for them to do but pray he remained alive until the airlift from Guam arrived. From there he would go to a hospital in Hawaii or if his family wanted to his home country for care.

They stopped by the on-call room long enough to bag up their wet clothing before they left the building.

"I'm starving," Landon said as they walked across the parking lot in the rain.

Macie stopped. "Where're we going? We don't have a car here."

Landon grinned. "I had a couple of guys who work in Maintenance go and pick up my car. Now, about food. We need some. Then bed."

"What?"

He spoke evenly. "We're going to have some breakfast before I take you home."

"Okay." Macie said nothing more as they climbed into the car. She must have been as dead on her feet as he was.

As he drove, she laid her head back and closed her eyes and only opened them when they arrived at his house.

"What are we doing here?" Her voice was higher than normal.

"Having breakfast. The one thing I do well in the kitchen is breakfast. Besides, nowhere's open this early. Even the hospital cafeteria doesn't open for staff for another thirty minutes."

Macie grunted as if she didn't care one way or the other. "All I want to do is sleep."

"Food first."

While he went to the kitchen, she wandered out onto the porch.

He called out, "Do you want vegetables in your omelet or not?" There was no answer. "Macie?" There was no answer. "Hello, Macie?" Still nothing.

Landon found her lying on the cushioned lounge on her side with her knees drawn up, her hands under her cheek, sound asleep. He smiled. Going to his bedroom, he pulled a light blanket off the end of the bed, then returned to the porch. He placed the cover over Macie and she sighed softly. His heart did too.

There were gray smudges under her eyes. His little heroine deserved a good rest. She'd done an amazing job that night, more than some would have dared. Landon gave her a light kiss on her forehead.

Sitting on the small couch beside her, he propped his feet on the coffee table, crossed his ankles, leaned back and overlapped his arms on his chest before closing his eyes. Food for him and his angel would have to wait after all.

CHAPTER SIX

MACIE WOKE TO the sound of rain tapping on tin. Opening her eyes, she recognized the porch at Landon's place and snuggled deeper into the blanket around her. The noise was comforting, and she watched the water dripping off the eaves for a moment.

What was that sound? Something clinked from far off. She knew that sound. It was whisking, and it was coming from the direction of the kitchen.

How long had she been here? With the grey day and no sun to judge by, she had no idea.

She pulled the blanket up around her face. Where had it come from? *Landon.*

"Hey there, sleepyhead."

He stood in the doorway between the porch and kitchen. His hair was damp and mussed as if he had just toweled it. She liked the look on him. His white T-shirt pulled tight across his chest, and she couldn't help but notice that he had a nice one. Well-worn jeans covered his lower half and his feet were bare. He was too sexy.

Last night he had been supportive, caring, professional. She couldn't have done what she had to rescue that man if she hadn't known Landon was there with her. When was the last time she'd had that type of security? It had been so long she couldn't remember. Maybe before the walls had come tumbling down on her father and their family? But even that had been false security. Last night she'd known Landon would do everything in his power to take care of her. That had been real. *He'd* been real.

"How about breakfast?" His focus remained on her as if he waited for her reaction.

She moved to get up.

Landon waved her down. "No, stay put. I was just checking to see if you were awake. Give me two minutes and I'll have it ready. You deserve breakfast in bed."

She didn't argue any further. He went back to the kitchen, and she slipped into the visitor's bathroom in the hall. She returned to the porch and found him waiting with two plates filled with toast, bacon and the most divine looking omelet she had ever seen.

Suddenly, she was ravenous. Her stomach punctuated it with a nice rumble of hunger. It seemed ages ago when they had eaten on the beach by the fire. "It smells wonderful. And looks just as good."

"Have a seat and let's eat." He picked up a plate and handed it to her.

She sat on the lounge and took it from him, then just as quickly put it down and jumped to her feet. "I forgot. I need to call the hospital to check on the man."

"I called half an hour ago. The weather has let up enough that the plane from Guam can get in. It's already on the way. He should be medevaced in the next hour. Now you need to eat. When you're done, I'll take you home. I'm sure you're ready to climb into a bed. I know that lounger wasn't the most comfortable thing for you to sleep on."

"I was too tired to notice." She took a bite of the eggs and savored the wonderful taste. Landon hadn't lied. He did make a fine omelet. "I bet you only feel that way after sleeping in your cushy bed while I was out here."

He patted the cushion next to him. "I slept right here beside you."

"You did. Why?" She tilted her head to the side and gave him a questioning look.

"I don't know. It just seemed like the right thing to do at the time. I sat down for a minute, and the next thing I knew I was sound asleep."

They ate for a few minutes in silence.

"You're a nice man, Landon Cochran."

"I appreciate that, coming from you. I know you haven't always believed that."

She shrugged and looked bashful. "Maybe that's true. But as time has gone by, you have proven yourself different."

Landon placed his empty plate on the table. "I know I've said it before, but I am sorry."

"I think I might have taken it harder because of what my father did. I felt like I had been lied to again and I was laying my anger at him on you." She hadn't realized that until this moment. Landon had made her no real promises. "I'm sorry I was so hard on you when you first came to the island. You really were great last night."

"I feel the same way about you." Picking up his coffee cup, he took a sip. "It certainly was an experience."

"Yeah, one I don't plan to repeat. I don't know what I was thinking when I said I'd go down."

"You weren't. You were just doing what had to be done."

"I don't even do climbing in general, much less narrow spaces." Her heart still beat faster at the thought of the danger she'd been in.

He grinned. "You didn't hesitate. I'd never have known you were afraid if you hadn't said so."

She fiddled with her fork. "An experience like that makes you feel lucky to be alive."

Landon's look met hers and held. His gaze dropped to her lips. He said softly, "Yeah, it does."

Macie's mouth went dry. She wanted to go to him, kiss him and then snuggle into his strong, reassuring body. To remind herself of why it was good to be alive. Instead, she stood with her plate in her hand and picked up his. "You cooked, so I should wash. Thank you for the meal— it was wonderful. Do you have other hidden talents?"

"No, just that one." The words had a solemn tone, as if he were disappointed in himself.

"I know that can't be true," she called over her shoulder as she went inside. Running water into the sink, she started washing the dishes.

A few minutes later Landon joined her. "I'll dry." He picked up a dish towel. "I had no idea you were so domestic."

She glanced at him. He was standing close, and she found that his warmth soothed her jumbled nerves. It felt too right to have him near. Her hand shook as she picked up a plate. "There's a lot you don't know about me."

"Is that so?" He watched her intently.

Something about his question challenged her. Made her feel daring. Or was that from the scare from the night before? Whatever it was, she wanted him. Wanted him to feel as out of sorts as she felt. Leaning her hip against the counter then turning toward him slightly, she grinned. "Yeah, that's so."

"Okay, let's play twenty questions." His voice held a dare.

"Twenty? That's too many. I've got to go."

"Okay. Make it ten. I'll start. What's your favorite color?" He sounded like a kid who had just gotten his way.

She returned to washing. "Blue. What's yours?"

"Green."

"All right. Favorite movie?" He stacked a plate in the cabinet.

She immediately came back with "Anything that ends in a happily-ever-after."

Landon pursed his lips in thought. "Really? That one I hadn't expected."

Macie placed their utensils in the holder to drain. "How about your favorite movie?"

"Any of the *Star Wars* films."

"Why am I not surprised?" She pointed to the stove. "Hand me that pan."

He picked it up. "Was that one of your questions?"

"No." She shook her head and took the pan from him. "I want to know…" She thought for a minute, then asked, "What was the name of your first dog?"

He grinned. "That one came out of left field. His name was Rufus. What was the name of your first boyfriend?"

She swung the washrag at him, sprinkling him with water. "Now you're getting personal."

His shoulders straightened with indignation. "And a guy's dog's name isn't?"

She huffed. "Steve. Satisfied? We were in the first grade. The baking pan, please. What's your favorite food?"

"I'll take a good juicy hamburger any day."

She laughed. "I should have known that. Nothing like a doctor who's heart smart!"

He bumped her with his hip. "I don't eat them all the time. They're more like my guilty pleasure."

"If you say so." Macie bet he ate more of them than he let on. This was too much fun. "What did you dream of being when you grew up?"

He shot right back. "A sheriff. I always liked Western movies."

"So, you have a hero complex? That came through clearly last night." She passed the pan to him to dry.

"You're one to be talking. You were the hero in my eyes. Do you think you'll always want to live in Saipan?"

She picked up the washrag, not looking at him. "I don't know. For right now it's the best place for me. Do you think you'll ever go back to just being a doctor?" She stopped what she was doing and looked at him. His back was to her as he hung the pan on a wall hook.

"Don't know. I've really gone a different direction now. The job in DC would be a desk job. If I get it."

"That's a shame. You're really good with the patients." Macie pulled the plug in the sink and watched as the water swirled down. She hated that his talent would be wasted. They sure could use him at the hospital. Would he ever consider staying in Saipan? Would she really want him around all the time? How could she possibly resist him then?

"What makes your heart flutter?" He folded the towel and neatly placed it on the counter.

She gulped. *Flutter?* "My heart flutter? What do you mean?"

His gaze met hers. "You know…pitty-pat." He put his hand over his heart and patted it with his palm. "You know…thump-thump."

Heat rose in her. She couldn't say it was him that made her heart flutter. "Puppies."

The look of astonishment on his face was comical before it turned piercing. Landon stepped closer. Her hand trembled as she placed the wet dishcloth over the divider of the sink.

"Really? That's the answer you want to go with?" His breath ruffled her hair.

He had her heart fluttering now. Turnabout was fair play. She faced him square on. "Hey, don't get ahead of yourself. It's my turn to ask a question."

"Shoot." His look didn't waver.

Did she dare ask? She felt more alive in the last few minutes than she had in years. She wanted more of that. If she asked the question, she'd have to accept the answer. Either way. She took a breath. "Would you like to kiss me and remind me of how wonderful it is to be alive?"

She didn't have to worry about the answer. Landon swept her into his arms, his mouth crushing hers. His lips were warm and firm. *Heaven.* She sank against him. Oh, yes, her heart was fluttering now.

Landon's mouth slanted across hers and then traveled off to follow the line of her jaw. She purred as she leaned her head to the side, giving him access to her neck. The soft, barely there brush of his lips made her shiver and heat pool low in her belly. When he kissed the hollow behind her ear she sucked in a breath and gripped his shoulders.

His mouth returned to hers. He demanded more. She moved closer, bringing her chest against his. Landon's hold tightened as his tongue caressed the seam of her lips in his request for entrance. With the skip of a heartbeat, she opened for him. His tongue joined hers, teasing, then insisted she join him in an erotic dance.

Landon turned her so that she stood between him and the counter. He pressed against her, his desire thick between them. Her arms circled his shoulders when her knees went weak so she wouldn't fall. His hands came to rest at her waist. Breaking their kiss, he stepped back and lifted her so that she sat on the counter.

She spread her legs and tugged him back to her. Once again, she'd stopped thinking about her actions and started living through his touch. Landon's lips found hers again as his hands slipped under the hem of the scrub shirt she still wore. Her skin quivered at the heat of his fingertips as they traveled across her skin.

"So soft. So perfect," Landon murmured against her cheek.

Macie's hands ran over his strong shoulders, following the muscles that had held her safe less than twenty-four hours ago. Her fingers moved on to his back. She nudged him closer. He resisted, taking her shirt and pushing it up to reveal her naked breasts. Macie squirmed, unsure about being so exposed.

"Please let me admire you. I've been thinking about you wearing no underwear the entire time we were eating." His words were almost a plea.

That knowledge sent heat rocketing through her. "Only if you remove your shirt so that I can do the same."

It took but seconds for him to jerk his shirt over his head and drop it to the floor. Placing a hand on his chest, she smoothed it over the hard plane, with its light dusting of hair.

Landon's finger touched her already extended nipple, making it harder. He circled it with his fingertip before cupping her breast in his palm. Lifting it, he took her breast into his hot, wet mouth.

Macie moaned. Molten desire pooled heavy at her center and throbbed forming a knot of aching need. When Landon sucked on her nipple, her fingers bit into his shoulders. She leaned her head back, closing her eyes as ripples of pleasure rolled through her. His other hand palmed her lonely breast. His tongue twirled around her nipple again, causing her hips to flex forward.

She wanted Landon with all that was in her.

He pulled slowly away, letting her nipple slide out between his lips, then he kissed the slope of her breast. "I've found something you like."

"Mmm…" Macie was in a sexual fog.

His mouth moved to her other breast and gave it the same attention as the first. Macie pulsed with want. She needed, needed…

Landon's mouth traveled up to her shoulder, where he dropped a kiss before continuing to her neck then finding her lips. "Put your legs around me."

She did and his hands cupped her bottom and he picked her up. He headed down a short hall and into the master bedroom. Her center rode along his hard length, teasing her heat as he walked. At that moment she would have gone anywhere with him.

Landon leaned down and pulled back what she guessed was the bedcover, then laid her on the soft mattress and settled himself over her. As his tongue ravished her mouth, one of his hands fondled her breasts. She pulled him closer, giving as good as she got.

Macie had been fighting her attraction to Landon since the moment she'd seen him again. It had all been building to this time and place. The life-and-death situation last night had only heightened her awareness. Being with Landon meant feeling alive.

His hand left her breasts and skimmed over her middle and lower half. Too soon, or not soon enough, he cupped her center. She lifted her hips, wanting more. Frustration built because the material of her pants prevented him from giving her what she desired. Her hands squeezed the muscles of his back, begging.

Landon's gaze met hers. His eyes had turned dark with desire. Seconds later his mouth found hers while his fingers went to the band of her pants. "These need to come off. I want to see all of you."

She lifted her hips, and Landon pushed the pants along her legs and down to her feet. She kicked them off.

He stepped far enough away that he could admire her. "You're beautiful. Amazing, in fact."

Macie couldn't help but blush. The few men she'd been with had never looked at her like Landon did now. Even during their first time he hadn't taken the time to look at her as he was now. It scared her and empowered her at the same time.

Quickly, he brought his body alongside hers again. She could feel his heat. He kissed her tenderly, and his hand cradled her breast and teased her nipple before his fingertips trailed a line over her belly and then lower, to where she craved his touch the most.

His mouth moved to one of her breasts as his hand ran long the top of her thigh to her knee, then followed the seam of her legs up again. He raised his head and looked at her. "Open for me, Macie. I want to touch you."

She relaxed her legs. His gaze didn't leave hers as his finger found her center, and she jumped as his touch sent a quiver through her. Still, his scrutiny didn't waver. He continued to tease her opening but didn't enter.

She moaned and lifted her hips. Offering. Begging. Her fingers dug into his shoulders. Anticipating.

Finally, Landon's finger slipped inside her. She closed her eyes, feeling the pleasure build, while Landon swept his mouth over hers again. Using her hips, she pushed into his hand. He continued to thrust and retreat, even finding her special spot.

The heat grew into a spiraling column of need that

burned within her. She pulled at Landon, grappling for something to end this delicious torture that was almost more than she could endure.

Landon flicked her nub. What was holding her to the earth sprung loose, and she flew into the heavens and a cloud of bliss carried her out of herself.

Landon raised his head and watched as Macie found her release. Had there ever been anything more beautiful? Not that he'd seen.

Now he truly regretted all the time they had lost over the years, though he wasn't sure what made him think they would have stayed together that long.

Macie's eyes opened and a dreamy looked filled them. There was a hint of wonder there as well. She smiled at him as she ran a hand along his forearm. Maybe the feeling of pure pleasure he still felt at giving her pleasure would have kept them together.

Easing down, he lay beside Macie and watched her. He wanted to be inside her, desperately. He ached with need, but he'd never experienced a moment like this before and he wanted to savor it. The throbbing in him turned to pain. He needed her.

Macie cupped the back of his neck and brought his mouth to hers. Her kiss was gentle, appreciative, but soon turned suggestive as her tongue caressed his. That strong will he so admired in Macie transferred to the bedroom.

With reluctance, Landon broke away from her. He stood and shucked off his jeans, leaving them in a pool on the floor. Reaching for the drawer in the bedside table, he pulled out a small square package. Opening it, he quickly covered himself.

Macie spread her arms wide, tempting him to rejoin her. He accepted the invitation and slid over her body, enjoying the connection between them. She cupped his jaw and directed his mouth to hers. Her kiss was warm and tender. Moments later her mouth left his to place tiny nips along his collarbone while his length strained between them.

Had he ever wanted a woman more? Only that once in Hawaii. Still, this was different somehow. More mature. More binding. More special.

Moving over her, he positioned himself between her legs until the tip of his manhood rested at her entrance. He broke their kiss. "Are you sure this is what you want?"

"I want you. Now."

With muscles straining to keep himself in check against his natural desire to go to the hilt, he slowly entered her. Inch by excruciatingly pleasurable inch he drove into her. Macie's fingers gripped his hips, encouraging him.

A soft sigh brushed his ear as he filled her. She was liquid fire, tight and oh, so sweet.

Landon held himself there a moment, just enjoying the connection. Soon, the need to move overcame him and Macie followed his lead. Need turned to heat, and heat turned to frenzy as he plunged into her.

Macie squirmed and gasped beneath him. Her legs circled his legs and pulled him more securely to her so she could match his rhythm.

He sensed her building release as her arms tightened around his neck and she tensed and arched her body. "Landon," she breathed.

Making a final deep thrust, he found his own release and joined her in ecstasy. Heaven help him, he wasn't sure he would ever be the same again.

Sometime later he woke from the daze of satisfaction to find he lay sprawled across the bed. He was spent like he never had been before. His hand brushed her silky hair, and lifting a handful, he let it flow over his fingers. The next time he picked up more.

Eyes still closed, he rolled toward Macie and inhaled deeply, committing her scent to memory.

"What're you doing?" Her voice held a curious note.

"Smelling you," he stated matter-of-factly.

"Why?"

"Because smell is the strongest sense for memory."

"And you want to remember my smell?" She rolled her head just enough to open one eye.

"I want to remember you."

Her hand trailed down his chest. "I rather like touch."

"I do too." Landon rose to rest his head on his hand. The other he grazed over her hip. "But I find sound rather rewarding as well. Especially when you call out my name."

Macie groaned and covered her face with her arm.

"Hey." He lifted her arm. "I want to see you. You're beautiful."

She grinned. "I think you're milking this for all it's worth."

"Maybe so, but just so I don't leave anything out…" The tip of his tongue licked the curve of her breast, and Macie rewarded him with a quick intake of breath. "You taste good too."

Pushing his shoulder, she pulled the sheet over her. "That tickles. I need to get up anyway. I need a bath and some clothes of my own."

"Do you really want to go?" He hated sounding pathetic, but he wanted her to stay.

She sat up, taking the sheet with her. He didn't bother to move, grinning when she looked her fill. His manhood flickered to life under her perusal.

A slight grin formed on his lips. "You know, if you keep that up, I'll hold you here and have my way with you again."

She looked down at him. For some reason, he had the idea she was trying to distance herself from him.

"You think so?"

"I know so." He took her hand in his, interlacing their fingers.

"I don't know that this continuing is such a good idea." She tugged on her hand. He let go of it, and she clasped her hands in her lap.

What? He already wanted her again. "What's wrong all of a sudden? Talk to me, Macie."

She looked everywhere but at him. "Nothing."

"Come on. A few minutes ago you were smiling, and now you're not. What gives?" Anger built in him, and it was starting to show.

"Do you think you could cover yourself if we're going to have this conversation?" She glanced down at his naked form.

He wiggled his eyebrows and gave her a wolfish grin. "Can't stop yourself from admiring me, can you?"

Macie huffed. "I can too."

"I saw you checking me out a minute ago."

She blushed. "Please."

Having compassion for her, he flipped the blanket over himself, leaving only his chest visible. "Okay. What's eating you?"

"I can't do this." She waved her hand around.

"What? Talk to me? Have sex with me?"

She avoided his gaze. "Yes. No. I mean, get involved with you."

"Are we involved?" He'd not thought that far ahead.

He knew only that he desired her. Admired her. Wanted to be around her.

She pierced him with a look. One he didn't like. "When I have sex with someone, I consider myself involved. I'm not very good at one-night stands. You of all people should know that."

"You asked me to take you to bed."

She dropped her head and covered her face with her hands. "I'm sorry. I know I suggested this. I was feeling vulnerable after that horrible rescue, and I have to be honest…" She looked at him. "I'm sorry, Landon. I was looking for an outlet for my emotions. I used you. I shouldn't have. Please take me home."

Now he was really angry, and he could tell it was about to boil over. Maybe it was best she did go home. He *felt* used, and he didn't like it one bit. Was this how she had felt all those years ago? Was she trying to get back at him? "You're right. I should take you home."

By the time they had gotten in the car it was dark. Thankfully, he had to concentrate on the winding road. Macie sat stiffly beside him, her hands firmly together. For the life of him he couldn't figure out what had gone so wrong so fast between them. Especially when it had been so perfect just minutes before.

He'd never had better sex, and from what he could tell, it had been no different for Macie. Even now he still wanted her. If she said the word, he'd turn around and carry her back to his bed.

But she wouldn't do that. The determined set to her jaw made that clear.

When they arrived at her house, she was out of the car and at her door before he could climb out. He sat watching the house until her light came on. Driving slowly, he returned home, suddenly feeling very lonely.

He would discuss this with her tomorrow after they'd both had a good night's sleep. Maybe they would be in a better frame of mind, be more able to talk this out. They had to work together for the next few weeks, and he didn't want animosity between them.

Somehow, he'd have to keep it all business. The problem was he didn't think about just business when he was around Macie. Too often his mind went to touching, kissing and the wonder he'd seen on her face. He wanted to give her that again, and again...

CHAPTER SEVEN

MACIE DIDN'T KNOW what had happened. The past—and all its pain—had come streaming back. Her father's betrayal. Landon's disappearance. She couldn't go through all that again. She was becoming too attached to Landon, and he would soon be gone.

It was all an illusion anyway. He wasn't offering her forever. He would be leaving and she would be staying. So how could she let things continue? Permanence, a solid foundation, was what she was looking for. Something more than sex. With Landon, wasn't sex all it would ever be? He'd made it clear he wasn't offering more.

The rescue had been so intense, and she'd just wanted someone to hold her. Landon had been available. Yet there was more to it than that—she'd come apart so completely in his arms. Even this morning as she'd admired his amazing body, hers had heated in response. That spark that they had once known had quickly turned into a flame.

Then reality had hit her. She didn't want or have time for heartache. She wanted her life to stay as it was. She had it under control. That had taken her years to achieve, and she couldn't let go now. The problem was, it had all changed when she'd made the decision to go to bed with Landon. Now she wasn't sure she could get it back to normal, but she would try. She had no plans to repeat what had happened between them.

She crawled into her cool, lonely bed and wished...

The next morning, she arrived at work early, making sure she had left her office for the wards before Landon got there. By the time she returned, Landon's door was closed and she could only assume he was busy inside. She was dodging him. She didn't want to ask Tatiana about him, fearing she would see the emotions Macie could barely conceal. Not very adult of her, but there it was.

By lunch she still hadn't seen Landon. Maybe she would get through the day without doing so. Yet she missed him. His grin, his teasing, the way he challenged her, had so quickly become an important part of her life.

Her phone buzzed. It was Tatiana. "Landon would like to see you when you have a minute."

"Okay. I'll go over in a few minutes."

"You do know he doesn't bite?" Tatiana asked.

That's what Tatiana thought. Macie's hand went to her neck where Landon had slowly and exquisitely nipped her skin the day before. "I know."

A few minutes later she stood at his office door, ready to knock. Even now, heat filled her at the thought of seeing him. She shook her head. *No, no, no.* She just couldn't do this.

Macie tapped on the door. At Landon's response, she opened it but remained in the entrance, unwilling to step too far into his space. "Tatiana said you needed to see me."

The look of expectancy on his face soon changed to coolness. Like her, he appeared to have slept poorly. Seconds later, his face became neutral and held only an expression of professional politeness.

Things had been so good between them two days ago,

and she had changed all of that with one simple question. Why had she let it get out of hand? She knew better. They had shared the most intimate interaction, and here they were back to being strangers, as much as they had been when he'd first arrived on the island. She didn't like it but would remain strong. Somehow, she'd survive the few weeks he would be there.

"Tatiana has made appointments with all three of the council members you introduced me to the other night. I'd like you to go with me to those meetings, if you would. I know it's inconvenient and you have your own work, but you're a good liaison and your presence will ease my way through the door. You put a face on the hospital that I cannot."

"I had suspected you would want me to go."

He leaned back in his chair and stretched. "There's one this afternoon. Another one tomorrow morning and the other on Thursday. Can you arrange your schedule to be available?"

It ran through her mind to go to him and massage his aching shoulders, and it took an iron will not to. Landon had really gotten under her skin. She feared he had snuck into her heart. "I'll make it work."

"Okay. Great. Today's is at two. I'll see you here at one thirty." His attention returned to the laptop in front of him.

"I'll be ready."

Landon nodded and returned to his work. Apparently, their meeting was over and she had been dismissed. Already she missed Landon's ready smile. What was wrong with her? She couldn't have it both ways. Wasn't he doing what she'd wanted him to do?

A few hours later she stood beside Tatiana's desk when Landon came out of his office with his sports coat hooked on one finger and slung over his shoulder. He wore a crisp light green shirt that made his eyes stand out and khaki pants. Everything about him said casual, confident, professional. He was so handsome it almost took her breath away.

He gave her a smile but his eyes remained cool. She'd hurt him. Deeply.

Macie tried to swallow the lump in her throat. She didn't want this bitterness between them. Somehow, she had to fix things. If only she could bring herself to explain.

What would she say? That she was afraid she was falling for him? That she didn't want to be left again? That she wanted forever not a fantasy. That she...loved him?

Loved him? Did she love him? She couldn't. Why couldn't she? He'd proved more than once that he was a good man. Whatever the reason, she wanted to see that light burning brightly in his eyes again when he looked at her. She would take that for as long as she could have it. When he left, she'd have that to hang on to. To bring out and enjoy whenever she wanted.

If she didn't do something soon, she'd miss out on what little happiness she might have with Landon.

"Macie?" he asked with a questioning expression.

"Yeah?"

"Are you ready?"

"Sure." She followed him out the door.

They walked in silence side by side along the hall and out into the parking lot to his car, and moments later they were headed up Capitol Hill.

"You remember where we're going?" She kept her tone light and friendly. She would talk to him after their meeting.

"Yes. I've driven around enough now that I can find my way, I believe."

Which was another way of saying he didn't need her anymore. She sat quietly the rest of the way.

Not soon enough for her, Landon pulled into a parking space in front of the Municipal Building. He retrieved his jacket from the back seat and shrugged into it. It made him look only more amazing. She had it bad.

Her fingers tingled with the urge to run them along his lapels and kiss him for luck. After the way she had acted, she was sure he wouldn't appreciate that. He'd treated her with tender care and she'd thrown it back at him. She would make it up to him. Somehow.

Since they were going to a business meeting, she'd gone home and put on a sundress and dressy sandals, which gave her some confidence. She looked more professional than she would have in her usual scrubs.

As Landon fixed his collar, he said, "By the way, you look nice."

"Thank you." Relief flowed through her. He had at least noticed she'd changed. Those few simple words made a spot in the middle of her chest glow. Maybe all wasn't lost.

Without further discussion, they entered the building. Landon spoke to the receptionist, and she escorted them into the mayor's office, where they were greeted warmly by Mayor Luc Ramos.

After a few minutes of small talk and questions about the accident, Landon presented his ideas for improvements at the hospital, spending a long time discussing the scholarship idea. He also explained his concerns for the hospital and how they would adversely affect the island if they weren't cleared up, and he finished with why she and Landon were there and what he would like the government to do to support the hospital, reminding Ramos of what quality medical care meant to the islands and the economy.

The mayor seemed to react positively to their ideas. Macie became concerned only when he questioned the hospital's ability to attract and hold on to consistent and appropriate leadership to see the plan through.

"We need new nurses and doctors, but if the leadership changes constantly, we can't offer anybody any incentives to live here. I see this as the largest need. Do you have any ideas in that direction?"

Landon spoke with authority, clearly having expected the question. "Not outside of offering financial incentives, which will be based on fulfilling a contract to stay for a minimum length of time."

The mayor nodded. "And I think we need someone who is not only committed to the hospital, the island and the surrounding islands in the senior role, but who also wants to make this their home, not just use it as a springboard for their next promotion." He gave Landon a pointed look. "Do you know someone who could fit the bill?"

Macie looked from one man to the other. Landon had all the right skills for the job, but his eyes were firmly on the job in Washington.

"I will make your concerns clear to my board and share your suggestions. With my organization's help, I believe you will find that person. We would evaluate every applicant carefully."

Mayor Ramos stood and offered his hand. "I know you will, and I offer my support for what I have heard so far. Thank you for coming."

Landon shook his hand. "Thank you, sir. You have my assurance that I'll see you get a quality administrator."

A few minutes later she and Landon were in the car.

"I think that went well." Landon wore a broad smile, the first real one she'd seen since she'd left his house.

"I do too."

For the first time that day, Landon truly looked at her. "Thank you for helping. I think having your seal of approval makes all the difference."

She returned his smile. "And I think you give me too much credit."

Landon started the car and drove back to the hospital. He had impressed her with his ability to concisely summarize a problem then offer a solution and project what things would look like if nothing was done and if his suggestions were implemented. It was an effective way of getting people on his side. She could understand why he was good at his job and was up for a promotion.

Everything about Landon appeared above reproach. Unlike her father. So why did she continue to have trouble accepting that? Landon wasn't a man who kept secrets or conducted business in an underhanded manner. Yet she had thought that about her father as well until she'd learned the truth.

"One down, two more to go," Landon said as they arrived at the hospital. "Tomorrow's meeting is at nine in the morning. Should I just pick you up at your house?" They got out of the car and headed inside.

"That'll be fine. It'll be nice to have a morning to sleep in."

"Okay. I'll see you at eight thirty."

"Landon, about yesterday—"

"Macie, you made yourself perfectly clear yesterday. Let's not rehash it. I have a job to do here and only a few more weeks to do it. If you don't mind, I'd like to concentrate on that."

His words were like a shot to her chest. She stood there, hoping her knees would remain stable. They'd made such a good team in the mayor's office, in the tanker, figuring out a plan for the hospital moving forward, and now he could hardly look at her. She'd messed up big-time. She'd let fear rule her. Her stomach roiled. There must be some way to get through to him. To get them back to the friendship they'd once had.

She watched Landon walk away and felt bereft. If she went after him, would he listen? She had to give him time, which left her standing there with her heart aching.

The next morning Landon picked her up, and they made the trip back up to Capitol Hill. Once again they had a fruitful discussion with another mayor who had already spoken to Mayor Ramos. This mayor was in agreement with Landon's plan , but also believed solid leadership would be necessary to make a difference.

As Landon drove down the hill, he commented as much to himself as to her, "Getting the correct administrator will be the key."

"I think I mentioned that was a problem the first day you were here."

He raised his brows. "Would that be an 'I told you so'?"

"Well, maybe, but an unintentional one. But a fact nonetheless."

"Point taken. I'll start compiling a list of requirements and let my boss know. He'll notify the board and see if they might have someone in mind."

At least they were being civil, she thought, though when he had picked her up that morning, he had greeted her with one of those smiles that didn't reach his eyes.

"Don't get too far ahead. We still have another mayor to see and the governor as well."

"I didn't have Tatiana make an appointment with the governor."

"Do you mind thinking outside of the box on that one?" She climbed out of the car.

"No. What do you have in mind?"

"Let me check on something and get back to you."

"Okay. Now I'm really curious." He walked beside her on the way inside. "I'm going to recommend to the hospital board that you be in on the vetting of a new administrator. Especially since you've been in on the ground floor with the new ideas."

"Thank you. That would be nice." At least he hadn't lost his professional respect for her.

They entered their office area together.

He stopped and looked at her. "Thank you for your help this morning. Your presence makes all the difference."

"I'm glad to help. This is something I believe in."

He continued to study her as if he were thinking, *But you can't believe in me?* Finally, he nodded and went into his office.

Even with Landon saying nothing she felt sick. What she'd had—could have had—she'd let slip through her fingers. When he'd left her in Hawaii, she'd not felt this miserable.

Macie wanted to scream.

Landon hadn't felt this ill since he was a child. His stomach was rolling like the giant waves that bashed the rocks at Banzai Cliff. His head pounded as if a jackhammer was running inside it and he was on fire. Somewhere he had picked up a virus. One that was kicking his butt.

He had called the hospital the day before and told Tatiana that he would be working at home that day. This morning he couldn't even get out of bed to call in because he was so weak. He'd spent most of the night going between his bed and the bathroom. He'd finally ended up just lying on the bathroom floor. More than once he'd tried to force some water down to keep from becoming dehydrated, but that hadn't gone well either. In his delirium, he'd thought if someone would just shoot him like they did horses when they went down, he'd be better off.

He groaned. To make matters worse, he was in the tropics, where it was steamy and hot half the time. He had just enough presence of mind to know that a storm was building. Having a fever didn't help. He dripped sweat.

What could be worse?

He could hear tapping. He closed his eyes. Maybe it would go away.

There it was again. He rolled to his side, putting his cheek against the cool tile of the bathroom floor.

"Oh, my heavens, Landon. Are you all right?"

Was it Macie? He had lost his mind. She didn't care about him. Didn't want his kisses, his loving. Why would she be here? He opened one eye enough to see a fuzzy version of her. The light hurt. He closed it again. "Go away."

"I can't do that."

She sounded so close. Worried. It had been a long time since someone had been concerned about him. He was the one who took care of people. His mother, his brother and sister, patients, hospitals.

"We have to get you to the bed." Macie pulled on his arm then tried to put hers under his back. "Landon, Landon. You're going to have to help me. You're too heavy for me to carry."

"Stay here." Why didn't she just leave?

"No! Now, help me get you up or I'll have to call for help." She pulled on him again.

Nope. He wasn't going to face that humiliation. Macie seeing him so sick was enough.

He moved to his hands and knees with more effort than he would ever admit to. Macie grabbed him around the waist as he pushed himself up to sit on the toilet. With great effort and Macie's help he managed to get to his feet. She grunted when he leaned heavily on her as they worked their way to the bed and fell on it. That was all he could do. His eyes closed and she lifted his legs and placed them on the mattress.

"Shift over. You don't want to roll off." Macie pushed at his hips.

He moved closer to the center but only because she did most of the work. "You can go now."

"Not going to happen" came her clipped return.

He didn't have the energy to argue with her, so he closed his eyes and drifted off into painless sleep.

The next time he woke it was to something cool on his head and somebody brushing his hair back from his forehead. Everything about it felt wonderful. He was still on fire, but the touch made it bearable. He moaned.

"Landon, you need to wake up. You need some medicine and to drink something."

He knew that voice coming down the tunnel. More than once he'd heard it in his dreams. *Macie.* Macie was here? Was he dreaming?

"Come on. You've got to sit up." She put an arm behind him, lifting him forward.

Something cool touched his lips.

"Drink."

He licked his lips.

"Good. Now I want you to swallow this pill." She pushed it into his mouth.

He shook his head. "Throat hurts."

"I know you're miserable, sweetheart, but you have to swallow this if you're going to get better." She gave him more water.

He coughed but forced it down.

"Take another swallow." The glass returned to his lips.

He didn't make any effort. It was just too hard.

"Just one more," Macie begged.

He did as she asked then dropped back on the bed and closed his eyes.

The next time when he woke it was to a cool, damp cloth moving across his chest. The hammer in his head had eased and his eyes no longer felt like salt had been poured into them. He still didn't think he could stand, but that didn't matter. He was happy right here with that cloth cooling his body. He sighed. Something pressed against his forehead. Lips, perhaps? Then sleep overtook him.

When he next became aware of anything it was someone shaking him awake. He'd been dreaming. He lay on the beach with Macie next to him. She held his hand as he listed to the waves. Rising over him, she leaned down and softly kissed him then moved away. He reached out to bring her back.

"Macie?"

"I'm right here."

Landon opened his eyes to see her above him. He made an effort to touch her, but his hand was too heavy and fell back to the bed.

"How're you feeling?" Her voice sounded so sweet and caring.

His eyes focused. "You're here."

"Yes."

His mind cleared. She was *here*. He was sick. "What are you doing here?"

"Nursing you. When you didn't show up for the meeting with the mayor, I knew something was very wrong. I came to check on you." She picked up a glass. "Here, you need to drink."

She held his head as he drank and swallowed half a glass. It tasted so good. "Thanks." The word sounded rusty.

"Lie back and go to sleep while I get you something to eat."

He looked beyond her to the window. It was dark. "What time is it?"

"Around nine o'clock."

He groaned.

"You've been asleep for hours."

"Last thing I remember was something cool moving over my chest."

Macie brushed a strand of hair out of her face. She looked tired. "I had to get your fever down. It broke a couple of hours ago. Now we need to get some food in you."

"Thank you." The words trailed off as he closed his eyes. He listened to the sound of Macie leaving him and going in the direction of the kitchen. He couldn't see her, but it was comforting to know she was there. She returned a few minutes later, and he opened his eyes to watch her. He liked the way she moved.

"Good. You're awake." She carried a bowl and a glass. Placing them on the bedside table, she stood above him. "Before you eat, do you need to go to the bathroom?"

He did but he didn't want her to help him, though he didn't think he could stand up by himself. "I can take care of that myself."

"I doubt that. Come on. I'll help you."

"I really—"

"No more arguments. You don't have anything I haven't already seen. Now, put your arm around my neck and let's go so we can get you fed."

She made it sound as if he was like any patient she'd ever had. He wasn't sure he liked being relegated to just anybody. Still, he did as she said.

Macie put her arm around his waist and they made it to the bathroom. In truth, he was glad of her help. "I can handle this part by myself."

"Since you're so squeamish, I'll just stand behind you and not look." Her hands remained firmly at his waist.

He'd been completely humbled in front of the very woman he wanted to impress. So much for his ego.

She helped him back to the bed.

"You do know I'll get you back for this," he grumbled.

"For what? Being the perfect nurse?" she asked sweetly.

"That and seeing me at my weakest."

She helped him to sit back against the pillows she'd piled behind him along the headboard. "Hey, we all have a time when we need help."

Had she ever really had one? She always seemed so self-sufficient, so self-assured.

"Seriously, you can go now. Just leave me alone and let me die in peace." Had she murmured something about men and their sickbed dramas?

"You're not going to die. You've just caught what we call the Pacific Grunge. Now, sit up and let me get something into you."

"What happened to the sweet nurse with the lovely bedside manner? Now you've turned into Nurse Iron Panties."

She chuckled. "It went out the door when I realized

how sick you were. Why didn't you call me and tell me you were so sick?"

He glared at her. Like he would have admitted that. Especially after the way she had left him on Sunday.

Macie's mouth formed a line and she nodded. "Got it. The great Dr. Cochran can't show weakness. I won't tell anyone."

It was more like he didn't what her to know just how hurt he had been after they'd made love. Or how badly he wanted her back in his arms. Or just how weak he was where she was concerned.

She perched on the side of the bed and picked up the bowl.

"I can feed myself."

She lowered her chin and gave him a doubtful look. "So you're willing to spill this lovely warm soup all over you to prove you're a man?"

Waiting a beat, she filled the spoon and put it to his lips. He slurped it in. The warmth felt good going down his raw throat. She offered him more and he gladly took it.

"I've not had someone feed me since I was a kid." He'd not thought of that in a long time. Most of his memories of his mother were negative or troubled ones. He'd been the caretaker for so long, he'd forgotten what it was like to be on the receiving end.

"My mother used to stop what she was doing—all her fund-raising duties and social obligations—when one of us was sick." Macie pinched her mouth closed as if she'd said something wrong.

"Us?"

"I have a brother and a sister too."

"Really? You've never mentioned them before. May I have a drink?"

She handed him the glass, but her hand hovered nearby in case.

"Where do they live?"

"Jean lives in California and Rob in New York. We couldn't stay in Chicago."

"Because of your dad?" He watched her closely.

Macie nodded as he studied the spoon she'd just filled so carefully.

"Do you ever talk to them? Your parents?"

She acted as if she had to think about that. "I talk to my mom pretty regularly. My brother and sister on holidays and birthdays."

"Your dad?"

The spoon clanked against the bowl. She put the bowl down and stood. "You need to finish all that water while I get some medicine. I'll be right back. I want all the water gone by the time I return." Nurse Iron Panties had returned.

Macie made it to the door before he said softly, "Your dad?"

She turned and faced him, her legs spread as if preparing to fight. "I haven't seen my dad since the trial. He's in jail anyway."

CHAPTER EIGHT

MACIE BRACED HER HANDS against the kitchen counter and hung her head. If she wasn't careful, she would be sick too. Why had she let Landon push her into saying that? Why did she need him to know? So he would realize what type of person she was? That she held a grudge. That when someone hurt her, it festered inside her. That he'd hurt her one time—unintentionally, but he'd hurt her nonetheless—and she just couldn't let it go. Couldn't easily give her trust. That she lived in fear of not seeing the true person behind their actions.

Taking a deep breath, she fortified herself to return to him. Shaking out a couple of pills into her palm, she went back into the bedroom. Landon had already slid down on the pillows and closed his eyes. The glass sat on the bedside table with most of the water gone. There was just enough left for him to take the medicine.

"Landon, don't go to sleep yet. You have to have this."

His eyelids lifted slowly. She picked up the glass and placed the pills in his open palm. Without complaint he swallowed them and handed the glass back to her.

His beautiful green eyes disappeared once again. "Thanks for taking care of me."

Macie looked down at him and saw he'd gotten some color back in his face. His hair went every which way, but she knew how soft it was. The stubble on his jaw gave him a dangerous appearance, the type that always made her heart beat just a little faster—flutter, as he would say. The man, even in his illness, did something to her.

He hadn't wanted her to see him vulnerable. Had it been necessary for him to hide any weaknesses for so long that he now couldn't? She had no doubt if she hadn't come to check on him, he wouldn't have called for help. What was it like to never open up to anyone? To always have to be the strong one?

She gave him a kiss on the forehead. "I'll never tell anyone how much you needed me."

She carried his bowl and glass into the kitchen and put them in the sink. She ate her own soup standing up at the counter. Finished, she washed the dishes and straightened up the kitchen before going to check on Landon. He slept peacefully.

Planning to stay the night to look after him, she needed something to sleep in. She rooted through his T-shirts in the chest of drawers, then pulled one out. She went to the bathroom to dress and slipped the shirt over her head, leaving her panties on beneath. It would be long enough on her to make her presentable if she had to get up in the middle of the night.

On the way to the living room she pulled Landon's door closed, leaving just enough space so she could hear him if he woke. Lying down, she tugged the blanket off the back of the sofa and covered herself. She had been busy and worried by the same measure, and she fell asleep right away.

Macie woke with a jerk. There had been a noise. Slinging the blanket off, she headed to Landon's bedroom. He wasn't there, but she could hear water running in the bathroom. He shouldn't be up without help. What if he had fallen? She hurried to the door and opened it.

"Landon, what are you doing?"

There was no response. She stepped inside. "Landon?"

"What?" He stuck his head outside the shower.

"What are you doing? You're too weak. You could fall. You should have called me." The man was trying to make her crazy.

"I needed a shower." His head returned inside the curtain.

She moved farther into room. "I know you did, but you should have let me help you in here."

"You're here now."

"How are you feeling?" She sat on the toilet seat, waiting impatiently.

"I'm fine. Better now that my fever has broken and I'm getting a shower."

Neither of them said anything for a few minutes.

"Landon, please get out. If you fall, I can't lift you." She stood, panic filling her at the possibilities of what could go wrong. Even a busted head was more than she could stand at this point.

He didn't answer her. Unable to endure it any longer, she pulled the curtain back. "Get out now."

Landon was leaning against the wall, and he had gone pale.

"For heaven's sake, Landon." She stepped in and turned off the water. Wrapping an arm around his waist, she led him out of the shower. "Sit." She helped him onto the toilet. Supporting him, she grabbed a towel off the rack and started drying him.

He shivered. She put a hand to his forehead. No fever. That was good, but he had the chills.

She finished drying him. Pulling the other towel from

the rack, she wrapped it over his shoulders. "Okay, Superman, let's get you back in bed."

"Not feeling all that super right now."

Macie helped him to stand, and he placed his arm over her shoulders. "I can believe it."

Slower than she would have liked, they made their way to the bed. Landon had become more dependent on her the farther they walked, and he dropped rather than sat on the bed.

She pushed his hair back. "No more getting out of bed without calling me for help."

"Yes, ma'am," he murmured as his eyelids lowered.

"You lie right here on this side of the bed. I need to change the sheets before you go to sleep." She pulled the blanket up over him and tucked it in close. "I'll be right back."

Once the bed had been changed and he had swallowed another pill, she tucked the blanket more securely around him. "In the morning you should feel a lot better. You just have the Pacific Grunge. You get it from not being used to the food, water or weather. Or all three."

He handed the glass back to her. "I'm cold. Keep me warm."

She wanted to lie next to him, to comfort him. She was tired too, and she thought how nice it would be to sleep on a bed instead of the sofa. Refusing to question her decision, she slipped under the covers and placed her head against his shoulder and an arm across his waist.

Landon exhaled and murmured, "I like you in one of my T-shirts. Especially when it's wet."

Macie sucked in a breath. The man had been ogling her. She grinned. He wasn't so sick he hadn't noticed her, which was good news. It would hurt when he left but she would deal; she'd just have to.

She snuggled closer and joined him in sleep.

* * *

Landon woke to the room bright with sunlight. From the direction of the beam he could tell it was late afternoon.

He felt better—weak, but better, though his stomach was rumbling fiercely. If he could get something to eat, there was a chance he would feel more alive.

A pleasant warmth lay against his back. *Macie.* Her arm was draped across his waist and one of her feet rested over his. His manhood reacted to the knowledge. This was a good way to wake, whether well or sick. She'd been the perfect caregiver, but was that professional nursing or because she had feelings for him?

Despite the reaction his body had to her, he had other issues to see about. He was still too wiped out to consider lovemaking, even were she to want it.

He could vaguely remember taking a shower and needing her help to get back to bed. And the soft wet material of his shirt outlining her breasts. That part of the night he'd like to revisit, but right now, he was going to have to wake her to get help to go to the bathroom. He wasn't going to make that mistake twice. The last time hadn't been his finest hour. Macie had made it clear in no uncertain terms he wasn't to get out of bed without her help.

Looking over his shoulder, he said, "Macie, I need to get up."

"Huh?" Macie jerked to a sitting position. "Okay."

She scrambled out of bed. Her hair was a wild mess around her face and the hem of his navy T-shirt hit her at midthigh and the sleeves covered her elbows. His shirt had never looked better. Macie was adorable. And now another part of his anatomy ached that had nothing to do with his stomach.

She hurried around the bed. "How are you feeling?"

"Better, and I want food. I hated to wake you, but I

was afraid Nurse Iron Panties would come out and I need to go to the bathroom."

She chuckled. "I'm not that bad, am I?"

"Only when I get in the shower without you."

"I believe you are feeling better." Happy notes filled her voice.

"You do remember I'm buck naked under here?" He referred to the sheets.

"I think I can control myself," she clipped.

"I was being a gentleman."

"I appreciate that, but I'll survive."

He pursed his lips. "Now I think my ego is damaged."

"I doubt that. Let me see you to the bathroom, and if you're steady enough, I'll leave you to get something for you to wear."

They made it across the room without mishap, Landon looking stronger than he felt. He didn't have to lean on her the entire way, yet she kept a hand on his arm all the same.

"Don't fall," she said as she left him to his business and went in search of something for him to pull on. She returned with a pair of his sport shorts. "Do you need help getting them on?"

He glared at her. "I do not."

She grinned and raised a brow. "You're getting feisty now."

He pulled on the shorts as she picked up the towel that lay on the floor and straightened the bathroom.

"I'll help you back to the bed." She took his arm.

"I've had enough of bed. I'd rather sit in the kitchen and watch you cook some eggs, bacon and toast."

"That's not going to happen. I think we should settle on something a little less aggressive. How about we start with some cheese toast? You can have something more substantial later."

He huffed. "Nurse Iron Panties is showing up again."

"Maybe so, but we need to make sure you don't have a relapse before we start filling your belly."

He took a seat at the dining table. To himself he had to admit he was glad to sit down again. Over the next few minutes he watched as Macie moved around the kitchen. She really was something. He wished he had the strength to show her how much he enjoyed watching the teasing sway of the hem of his T-shirt just below her temping backside.

She might have hurt his feelings, but he wasn't immune to her. Nothing had really changed about that. If anything, after the last few days, he was crazier about her than ever.

What if he let go and admitted his feelings for her? Both to himself and to Macie. What was the worst that could happen? He placed a hand on his stomach. It ached at the thought. He couldn't care that much; if he did, his life might be destroyed if she didn't feel the same. Everything he had worked for would be at risk. No, he couldn't allow that to happen. Landon had seen what that type of love could do to a person. He had no intention of letting another person destroy him like his father had his mother.

Macie turned to him. "How about a cup of hot tea?"

"I'd rather have coffee."

"Okay, but your stomach may not like it."

"I'll take my chances. Yesterday, I thought I was going to die. Nothing can make me feel worse than that." Except her not feeling the same about him as he did about her.

"A little dramatic, don't you think?" She placed bread on a baking sheet.

"I'm a doctor after all. I should know."

She went to the refrigerator and pulled out the cheese. "Isn't the saying that doctors make the worst patients?"

"There's old Iron Panties again. I prefer the warm, tender Macie curled up beside me." He needed to watch his thoughts and what he said.

Blushing, she went about making them some food. Soon, she placed a plate of toast in front of him and one in her spot. She brought over coffee and a glass of water for him and a mug of tea for herself. They ate in silence.

To his great relief, the toast settled in his stomach without any negative reaction. When he finished the second piece, he leaned back and held his coffee cup. "Thanks for coming to my rescue."

"You're welcome. No matter how strong you guys think you are, you still need support when things aren't going your way."

He took a sip of his drink. "That's an interesting way of putting it. I think there's something behind that."

Shadows filled her eyes.

"What happened?"

Macie blinked, surprise now in her eyes. Was she amazed he'd seen the shadows? She didn't say anything, just watched him. He recognized the second she made up her mind. "When my father was on trial, he wanted us to all be there. Standing behind him. Supporting him even though he'd taken all those people's money. The media followed us everywhere. They even came to the hospital when I was trying to work, yet my father showed us off like everything was all right."

Landon set his mug down. "That must have been difficult and more than a little humiliating."

"It was. Very. That's why I went to Hawaii. To get away." She wasn't looking at him. Instead, she twisted her napkin, something he'd learned she did when she was nervous. "About the other day—I know you must think I'm a tease."

"I don't think that. I understand now. It's probably for the best."

"Still, you deserved better. I tried to tell you that on Monday but you didn't want to hear it. I was scared."

"Scared?" That wasn't what he wanted her to feel. "I didn't hurt you, did I?"

"No, I'm not talking about physical hurt." She pointed to her chest. "I'm talking about me liking you too much."

There it was. Not what he wanted to hear, yet also what he wanted to hear so very much. His heart swelled. She did like him. "That's a bad thing? There has always been a spark between us."

"I know. It's just that I don't know where this is going."

Macie did sound scared. "I won't make you any promises. I've already told you I don't do forever. Never plan to. What I would like very much is to enjoy the here and now. Couldn't we just be good friends and make the most of that while I'm here?"

"I'm not very good at trusting people. Or taking them at their word. My father saw to that."

He reached across the table, placing his hand over hers. "I won't disappear on you ever again, Macie. I'm not your father. You *can* trust me."

She gave him a wry smile.

Landon had hoped for more than an unsure smile. Why? Didn't he just want a good time, nothing more? He'd let her think about whether or not she could trust him. He couldn't even imagine what it had been like for her to endure what her father had put her through. Then he'd come along and left her like he had in Hawaii. No wonder she was unsure about relationships. She'd been disappointed one too many times. He would make sure he never hurt her again.

"What time is it?" he asked, looking toward the clock on the kitchen wall.

"Four o'clock."

He started to stand. "I need to call the hospital. Check on things."

"I told Tatiana yesterday that we were working from home today. Everything is fine or someone would have called. What you need to do is go back to bed and get some rest."

He grinned. "And there's Nurse Iron Panties again."

"Maybe so, but the only way you're going to be well enough to meet with the governor by Sunday afternoon is to rest."

He sat straighter. "You got us an appointment?"

"Of sorts." She picked up the plates and started toward the kitchen.

"What does that mean?"

"It means I hope you like to fish." She put their dishes in the sink.

His lips pulled tight. "We're going fishing with him?"

She looked back over her shoulder. "We're going to his favorite fishing hole, where we'll 'accidentally' run into him."

"Macie Beck, I had no idea you were so sneaky."

She grinned and shrugged. "What can I say?"

"You can say you'll come watch a movie with me. I'm not sleepy." He picked up his water and drank it all. "See, I'm following the nurse's orders." He set the glass down with a thump.

Turning away from him, she stood beside the sink. "All right. Let me straighten up in here."

By the time Macie joined him, he had a movie queued

up and ready to go. She pulled the chair that sat in the corner over to the bed.

"Hey, what are you doing?"

"Getting a seat," she answered as if he had asked a stupid question.

"Come up here beside me. Be a friend." He patted the bed. "I promise not to attack you. I don't have the energy even if I wanted to."

Macie looked from the bed to the chair and back. "The bed does look more comfortable." Propping a couple of pillows against the headboard, she sat and leaned back against them, leaving as wide an expanse between them as possible.

"I hope you like suspense."

"I do. Very much."

"Then I think you'll like this one." He clicked the remote and the movie began playing.

They were into the film only a few minutes when he looked over to find Macie asleep, her chin resting on her chest. Smiling, he put his arm around her shoulders and brought her closer, letting her head rest on his shoulder. She rolled to her side, her hand coming to sit over his heart. With the movie droning on, he closed his eyes and drifted off to sleep. If he must be sick, this was the way to do it.

Macie woke to a late evening stream of light coming through Landon's bedroom window. The brush of a hand over the outside of her thigh shot a tingle of awareness to her center. The touch went farther up then slowly down again.

She lay curled against Landon's side, her hand on his chest. She nuzzled against him. He trailed kisses across her forehead. She looked up at him. His gaze met hers, a flame that had nothing to do with a fever or friendship flickering brightly in his eyes. Landon wanted her. He kissed her, his lips tender and questioning as if he were holding back, unsure of his welcome.

Macie had to make it clear that she wanted what he could give while she could have it. He'd made it clear where he stood and she believed him, and she still wanted him anyway.

She ran her hand up to circle his neck and opened her mouth. He might break her heart, but she wanted him and she wanted him to know it. She said against his lips, "Should we really be doing this? You've been sick. You're weak."

"I'm not that weak." He took her hand and ran it over the length of his arousal. He gave her a wicked grin. "But it might help if you did most of the work."

Her blood raced and pooled at her center. She smiled. "What do you have in mind?"

"Climb up here and I'll show you."

He pulled her leg over him and she shifted so that she straddled him. "Like this?" she asked.

"You're getting the idea." He reached out and cupped her breast. "So perfect."

She ran her hot center over his hard length. "You'll tell me if it's too much for you."

Landon groaned. "I don't think that's gonna happen."

She giggled.

His palms came to rest on top of her thighs, then slid along them before going under the hem of her shirt. His thumbs made little circles over her skin. She hissed as tingles zipped through her. Landon's look locked with hers and held. His hands moved higher and she lifted her hips. One of his hands moved closer to her center. A finger traced the line of her panties and teased her. He pulled it away.

She whimpered her disappointment.

"The panties have to go. I need to touch you."

Without breaking eye contact, she lowered her panties and kicked out of them. Landon licked his lips. She stepped to the bedside table, pulled out the drawer and removed a foil package.

Landon reached out a hand and cupped her backside, caressing it. She moved to climb over him again.

"Wait."

She stayed where she was.

Landon's hand left her bottom, and he rolled to the edge of the bed. Bending his arm, he rose up on an elbow and rested his head on it. "Now, come here please, and put your knees against the mattress."

Macie did as he requested.

Using his free hand, he drew a finger up her thigh, brushed her curls and drew it down the other leg. She quivered, thankful for the support of the bed.

"Let me touch you. I want to feel your heat so badly."

Her eyes met his. Desire filled and flickered in Landon's gaze. She throbbed for his attention.

"Please." His finger tracing down her leg was little more than a whisper of movement.

She shifted slightly, widening her stance.

With a lift to his lips, Landon leisurely ran his finger across her center.

Her legs shook. "Landon?"

"Shh. You're so responsive. I like how you answer my touch." His eyes moved to focus on his finger.

Placing her hand on his head, she gripped his hair, needing something to support her.

This time his hand went under the shirt to tease her

breast. She leaned into his touch. Goose bumps rippled over her skin as he brought his fingers down over her stomach and lower.

Macie bit her bottom lip. Wanting, needing, silently begging for more. For him.

Landon's hand found her center again, a finger entering her. Bending her knees, she pressed down on his hand. Her grip on his hair tightened. She wanted...

He pulled his hand back. She whimpered her displeasure and was rewarded with its return. Grinding against his hand, she wanted more.

"Look at me, Macie. I want you to know who's giving you pleasure. Who it is you can trust to be open and honest with you."

She studied his body for a moment. He might have been in a relaxed position, but every muscle was tense, as if coiled to spring. His manhood lay thick and extended, ready beneath his shorts. Her bright gaze met his smoky one. Landon moved his hand again, setting up a rhythm that she joined. Her knees sank into the mattress as she pulsed over his finger.

"Landon?" she whispered as her eyes widened, and that silver coil built and tightened within her.

He didn't blink. "Let it go, honey. I'll catch you."

She threw back her head, pressing hard into his hand, and soared into the power of her release. Landon caught her before her knees buckled, pulling her across him. Her heart pounded next to his.

Holding her, he rubbed her back and said soothing nothings against her ear. She was weak as a newborn kitten, and she'd thought he might not be strong enough to make love.

After a few minutes had passed, Landon said, "Honey, I need you."

Macie didn't move immediately, but soon she wiggled over him and drew down his shorts so that his length stood tall and proud between them. Finding the package she had dropped near his leg, she opened it and rolled it on him.

She rose onto her knees until his tip waited at her opening, then she slid her center over him. Her gaze found his. His eyelids were lowered halfway and his jaw was tight.

"Landon, look at me."

His eyes widened.

"I want you to see who's taking you." She glided down him.

Landon groaned. When she finally held him completely, he sighed, then began to move his hips. She placed a hand on his shoulder. "Nope. I promised to do all the work."

She raised herself onto her knees until she held only his tip, then plunged down again. She repeated the move until his hands gripped the sheet. Increasing the speed, her need grew. His hand circled her neck and brought her mouth to his. The kiss was so erotic she tightened around him and shook, but she never changed her rhythm.

Landon's hips rose in a hard lunge as he ended the kiss and grabbed her hips, holding her secure as he howled his release. With a wiggle of sweet pleasure, she joined him, then fell over his chest.

Macie smiled. As sure as the ocean waves hit the beach, she was in love with Landon Cochran.

Landon looked at Macie as she walked along the pier beside him on Sunday afternoon. She wore a baseball hat on her head, dark glasses and a tight-fitting T-shirt that hugged the curves of her breasts. The scoop neck of her shirt just covered one of his favorite spots to kiss, while her cutoffs allowed a beautiful view of her legs. Well-worn deck shoes protected her feet. The best part was that she wore a smile, one he was confident he'd placed there. He couldn't help but return it.

His recovery had been quick. He and Macie had spent all Saturday in bed watching movies, talking and making love. He had never shared a more fulfilling love life. Macie was everything he'd ever dreamed of.

He grinned.

She met his look. "What's that grin for?"

"I was just thinking, if I share my cure for Pacific Grunge, they might not believe me."

"That would be?"

He squeezed her hand. "Taking a lovely woman to bed."

Macie rewarded his teasing with a blush.

"I don't take care of all my patients in the same manner."

Landon raised his shoulders in a look of mock importance. "I certainly hope not. I like thinking I'm special."

It was her turn to grin. "Oh, you stand up and out… in a crowd."

His satisfaction grew at her innuendo. He appreciated the sassy Macie. "So exactly why are we going fishing?"

"Let's just say that the governor is a lot more approachable when he's outside with a rod and reel in his hand."

"He doesn't have his business meetings in his office?"

"Sure, he does. He's very official. But you're more likely to get his support and a yes by approaching him this way. You said we needed to have some tax breaks and an influx of money. He's the guy to give the hospital those, so we need him to agree. Fishing makes him agreeable."

"You're a devious person, Macie Beck. Remind me to stay on your good side."

"I like to think of it as being smart." She pulled her hat down a little.

"That too. So, what's the game plan?" He became more interested by the minute.

"Nothing special. Just sit down next to him and start fishing. Have a conversation."

He nodded. "Okay. That sounds reasonable."

She shifted the tackle box she carried to her other hand. "Do you fish?"

"Not often. It's been years." When he was a boy with his father. Those days were long gone. He'd not seen his father in a long time.

"Let's hope it's like riding a bicycle and you never forget how. Okay, focus now. See the man with the blue shirt up there on the left?"

"Yep."

"That's the governor," she whispered as if they were doing espionage.

Minutes later they sat on the pier with their feet hanging over the side. They had settled in and dropped their lines into the water.

Macie leaned forward, looking past him to the man sitting a few spaces farther beyond.

"Governor Nandos? Is that you?" she asked sweetly.

The stout middle-aged man looked at her. "Well, Macie. How are you doing?"

"Fine, sir. And you?"

His attention was on his line. "Great. Great. Any day is a good one when you get to fish."

Landon wasn't sure about that but he nodded his agreement anyway.

Macie waved a hand toward him. "Have you met our interim administrator, Dr. Landon Cochran?"

"No, I haven't." The governor looked at him.

"Nice to meet you, sir." Landon reached over and shook his hand briefly.

Macie looked at the governor again. "Are you catching anything?"

"A few. Not what I want them to be. But the day's young." The older man gave them a toothy grin.

The conversation tapered off for a few minutes.

Macie broke the silence once more. "Governor, I don't know if you know it, but Dr. Cochran has been doing an evaluation of the hospital. I've been assisting him in a number of areas. Together we've come up with a plan to build on what we already have."

"Is that so?" The governor started to pay attention to her.

"Yes, we have a couple of very inventive ideas."

"I don't usually talk business while I'm fishing, but I have to say you have pricked my interest. What are some of those ideas?"

Landon launched into their short but sweet preplanned speech.

The governor's face screwed up in thought. "I have to admit that sounds promising. Something that I could support. Put together your proposal and I'll give it a look."

"May I tell my board that you like the plan?" Landon dared.

"You may certainly tell them I'm giving it serious consideration. And if they agree to do their part, I'll do mine." His attention returned to his fishing.

Macie squeezed Landon's hand. He grinned at her.

Half an hour later, Macie stood. "At the rate we're catching fish we're going to starve. I think they're hiding from us today." She looked down at Landon. "How about buying me a burger?"

"Okay." He helped her gather up their equipment.

As they started to walk away, the governor said, "Giving up already?"

"Yep," Landon said. "Macie has decided on a burger instead of fish."

"Okay. I'll expect that proposal on my desk this week." The governor spoke more to the water than to them.

"It'll be there," Landon assured him.

As they walked back toward dry land, Macie grabbed his hand and swung it between them, taking a little skip. "We did it."

Landon grinned as a glow of pleasure grew in him. He could get used to this feeling, even though he knew it couldn't last.

CHAPTER NINE

ON MONDAY MORNING Macie and Landon returned to work. Tatiana had given her a questioning look when they'd entered the office area together, but Landon had immediately handed Tatiana a list of the information they needed.

After Macie saw to some nursing problems, she went to Landon's office to help him compile the proposal for the governor. They planned departmental meetings, staff meetings and changes that needed making. Positive ones. Landon had a knack for getting people to buy into a plan. Part of that was that he made them feel like they were partners instead of subordinates.

They rescheduled the visit to the mayor that they had missed while Landon was sick, and Landon apologized profusely for not being able to make the first one, bringing the mayor a bottle of the local drink to make up for it. The mayor was more than happy when they left.

Macie hadn't been this excited about life since before her father had destroyed her world. The only dark cloud in her happiness was that Landon would soon have to leave. His assignment had been for six weeks, and that was almost up. They didn't talk about it, yet they were both aware. More than once Landon had caught himself

before he said something. By the look on his face, she'd
known it had to do with him leaving.

A couple of times he'd taken calls in his office with the
door closed. He said nothing to Macie, but she had been
pretty sure they had been about the job he was trying to
get. She wanted the best for him, but she didn't want him
to leave. Landon didn't mention what was between them,
and she didn't ask. He also never said anything about his
feelings, but based on his actions he was as in love with
her as she was with him. The question was whether he
would allow himself to act on those feelings.

Her greatest worry was how they would ever survive
a long-distance relationship. She had to accept that her
heart would break. But she'd made a choice, and she
would have to live with it. The even sadder thing would
have been if she'd stood by her original plan and kept
him at arm's length. The happiness she had so far would
be worth all the heartache to come. This would always
be the most precious time of her life.

On Tuesday afternoon, two days after they had talked
to the governor, they were in his office working when
Tatiana rushed in. "Macie, you're needed in Emergency
right now."

"Why?"

"Something about the birthing clinic." Tatiana looked
anxious. "The EMTs are bringing in a mother and baby."

"Let them know I'm on my way." Macie stood.

Tatiana left.

"Birthing clinic? I had no idea there was one." Landon
had come to his feet as well.

"Can you come too? I may need your diplomatic skills.
I'll fill you in on the way." She headed for the door.

Together they hurried toward Emergency.

Macie spoke as they went. "There's a birthing center

in part of one of the closed resorts. They've taken a few of the rooms and made them into birthing areas. Chinese women—I guess it would be more like their families— pay an exorbitant amount, upward of fifty thousand dollars, to have their babies here."

"Why?"

"Because Saipan is a US territory. The babies are American citizens. They get a US birth certificate and passport. Those babies are called ABC babies—American-born Chinese. The laws are changing to control this but we do have a few that slip through."

"I had no idea that was going on." Landon sounded as surprised as she thought he might be.

"I didn't either until I started working here. There are travel agencies in China who make a business out of selling to the mothers. They have brochures and offer packages."

"The mothers must be from families with a lot of money to afford that." Landon's strides lengthened.

"Yes, most are from well-to-do families. The ABC babies make up a large percentage of the babies born on Saipan currently."

He shook his head. "Unbelievable."

"I have a few issues with this clinic which is run by a representative of the tourism company in China. Despite what he says, I don't believe the clinic offers the standard of care they advertise. Another issue I have is that the clinic is only prepared for healthy births. If something goes wrong, they don't have the equipment or the ability to handle issues. They're quite arrogant about what they do and don't care to have any type of relationship with the hospital. And mostly I just don't like the concept of paying for US citizenship."

"Amazing."

"I've had dealings with this clinic before and they're uncooperative. They believe if the word gets out that we were involved, it will hurt business. One case that came in, the mother was in such bad shape that by the time they called us, she'd spent weeks in the hospital. I think they are more interested in the bottom line than they are their patients."

"So why am I coming along?" Landon held the door open for her to enter the ER.

"In traditional Chinese culture they recognize a man's authority more than a woman's. I think you might help the mother and baby get the care they need with less hassle."

"Got it."

Thankfully, Landon was in a suit instead of scrubs. That would add to his look of power.

The ambulance was just rolling to a stop at the door when they arrived. They picked up the pace and went out to meet it along with the ER doctor and nurse. A Chinese man hovered nearby.

Macie touched Landon's arm. "That's the medical tourism representative. He'll act as if he doesn't speak English well, but he does. Last time he spent most of the time on the phone."

Landon nodded as he seemed to size the thin young man up. The mother coming by them on a gurney drew their attention. She and Landon joined the other staff members in an exam room.

The EMT gave a report. "Twenty-three-year-old Chinese female. Postpartum hemorrhaging, low BP. Patient has a history of smoking."

Macie groaned.

Landon raised a brow in question.

"They're supposed to screen the mothers. They have to

be drug-free and have never smoked." What she didn't say was that they would take anyone willing to pay enough.

The ER doctor was busy doing a uterine massage in an effort to stop the bleeding. "We need whole blood here stat."

"Heart rate going down," the nurse called.

The monitor warning bells went off. The patient had no heartbeat.

Macie and Landon stepped into action then. Landon started hand compressions on the mother's chest while the nurse worked at pushing medicine into the IV that the EMTs had placed. Macie pulled the crash cart close and prepared the defibrillator paddles.

"Ready?" she called. She checked to see that the ER doctor had removed his hands from the patient before handing the paddles to Landon.

He quickly took them and placed them on the mother's chest.

Her body jumped as the electric current flowed through her body.

"Nothing," the nurse stated.

Landon said, "Again."

Macie reset the machine. "Ready?"

Landon placed the paddles once more. This time there was a small beep as the heart returned to beating. A look of relief came over his features as he handed the equipment back to her.

"Let's get this bleeding stopped and get this woman to ICU," the ER doctor said. "She's going to have a long recovery."

Half an hour later, Landon and Macie watched as members of staff pushed the mother up the hall toward the ICU.

Landon looked around. "I want to talk to the guy from the clinic."

Macie wasn't so sure that was a good idea, but from the determined look on his face, now wasn't the time to argue with him. He was a man on a mission.

"There he is." Landon headed toward the outside door.

Macie followed, wanting to make sure no one over-stepped—she wasn't thinking so much about Landon, but about the other man. She'd had dealings with him before and was not impressed.

"May I speak to you a moment?" Landon asked the man.

He just looked blankly at Landon then back at his phone.

"I've been told that you speak English well. So please don't try to imply you don't." Macie recognized the tight notes in Landon's voice. He was controlling his anger.

The man shrugged and gave Landon a disinterested look. Landon told the man who he was but received no reaction from him.

"That mother back there—" Landon indicated with a thumb over his shoulder "—almost died from your com-pany's negligence. I'm still not sure she won't, and she might have brain damage. And there's a baby that has no one currently to see about it. You get on your phone and you let your bosses know that I'll expect them to take care of her bill and see that she has the care that she requires at home, or I will make it my life's mission to shut you—and all the other agencies like yours—down."

Macie's chest filled with pride. With the World Health Organization behind him he just might have the clout to make his words a reality. The man's eyes widened as Landon spoke. His haughty look had disappeared.

Landon glared at the man. "Is that understood?"

The man nodded.

Landon turned and walked away. Macie followed him with a smile teasing her lips. They stepped out of earshot of anyone else. She leaned in close to him. "That might have been the sexist thing I've ever seen."

Landon's shoulders relaxed. He met her look, a smile forming on his mouth. "You think so?"

"I do."

"Maybe I should go talk to him again." He moved to turn.

She grabbed his arm and shook her head. "I don't want you to single-handedly ruin our tourist industry by making China mad at us."

"Okay. I'll keep it together. Let's go check on the baby."

They strolled to the nursery. There they received a report that the baby was doing fine but just a little small. She and Landon stood over the bassinet, looking down at the newborn.

When the nurse had walked away, Macie asked, "Have you ever wanted children?"

"I used to, but that was a long time ago. Before I understood how they could be hurt by their parents. Would you like to have children someday?"

"I used to dream of having a houseful." She glanced at him. What she didn't say was *with you.*

"I think you would be a great mom." His words were almost a soft caress.

"Thanks, that's nice to hear. I would certainly try. I bet you would be a wonderful father."

"I don't know about that. I don't have any real knowledge of how to be a good one. I had some really poor examples in my parents." He turned toward the door.

She joined him. "I would never lie to my children."

"I'm sure you wouldn't." He gave her a sly grin. "Back to you thinking I'm sexy—"

"I knew I shouldn't have said that."

He winked. "Now that you have, how about showing me just how sexy you think I am tonight?"

She raised her chin in thought. "Maybe I could be talked into doing that."

"I think I can do that." His hand brushed hers.

Macie lightly swatted his arm. "I'm not that easy."

"No, and I like it that way." He looked around and, not seeing anyone, gave her a quick kiss on the lips.

On Friday evening, they were in his office working on a presentation to his board when Landon looked up at the clock. "That's enough for today. I had no idea it was so late. I've got to go. I promised my girl we would do something special tonight."

"I bet she'll understand if you're running late."

He went around the desk to stand beside Macie. Running the back of his hand down her cheek, he said softly, "You think she's that understanding?"

"I think she'll think you're worth waiting on."

One of the nicest things about Macie was that she made him feel special. He had rarely felt that type of regard from a woman. "Do you, now?"

He liked playing word games with her. She had a quick wit. "I tell you what. I'll go home and see that she's all dressed and ready to go."

"Okay. Tell her I'll see her in an hour."

Macie giggled. "She'll be ready. Can I tell her where she's going?"

"Nope. It's a surprise."

His phone rang. He checked the screen and saw it was a Washington number. This might be the good news he'd been hoping for…but that would also be the news that takes him away from Macie. "I've got to take this."

She nodded and gave him a little wave before going out the door.

As he pulled up at Macie's, she came out of her door as if she had been standing at a window watching for him. The idea that he had planned a date and wouldn't tell her about it had made her restless. Yet she wore the dress he had requested, the flowing yellow one with the flowers. The slim straps left most of her beautiful tan shoulders bare, and the dress hugged her hips. Everything about her made him feel good from the inside out. His chest tightened.

He swept her up in his arms, and she kissed him as if she hadn't seen him in days, not just a few minutes. This he would miss most of all. But for tonight he would enjoy every minute they had and deal with the rest tomorrow.

"Now, tell me where we're going?"

Landon chuckled. "Not yet. You'll see." He went around the front of the car and opened the door for her.

He drove along the beach road, going well past the lights of the city, until he saw the pole with the orange ribbon, where Joe had told him to turn off. It was little more than a path, but when he could see the water he parked the car.

"How did you find this place?"

"I asked Joe. One of his family members owns this land. He gave me permission for us to come here."

"Why, Dr. Cochran, you're becoming a regular islander. Networking and all."

"Maybe a little bit. I do know a few more people than I did." Landon opened the door. "This is where we get out."

Landon helped her out then went to the trunk and retrieved the picnic basket. Taking her hand, he led her down to the beach. There he was pleased to see that the firepit he had expected had been prepared.

"Just when did you do this?" Amazement filled Macie's voice.

Landon shrugged. "I might have had a little help. You won't let me out of your sight."

"You do have a healthy ego. I might have overdone making you feel important."

Landon couldn't imagine that ever happening. He barked a laugh. "It's more like keeping me humble."

When they reached the pile of wood, he spread a blanket out and started the fire, then helped her to sit. She looked so feminine sitting elegantly with her legs to the side and her hair softly blowing in the breeze.

He joined her on the blanket and pulled the basket close. "Let's see what we have in here."

Macie watched as if he were a magician and she was expecting him to pull a rabbit out of a hat.

"We have champagne." He handed her a flute that he had filled from a bottle. "And there's shrimp cocktail."

"Where did this all come from?"

"Joe again. His uncle is a chef at one of the resorts."

"I'm going to have to thank Joe."

Landon grimaced. "It was my idea."

"Oh, I plan to thank you." She gave him a sexy smile.

"That's more like. I'm always better when I'm appreciated." He pulled another bowl out.

"I thought I had made it clear more than once that you are appreciated," she said softly.

He gave her a long look. "I believe I should see what else is for dinner, or we won't be eating if you keep looking at me that way."

Macie's giggle circled his heart. He focused on pulling more seafood, fruit and raw vegetables, and bread from the hamper.

"Goodness, this is a feast."

"Yeah, I had him pack it full." Landon was pleased that he'd impressed her.

Landon raised his glass. "I'd like to make a toast. To a beautiful night with a beautiful girl."

"Thank you."

He clinked his glass against hers. They each took a sip. "As much as I enjoy the champagne, I am hungry." Landon secured his glass in the basket and pulled out plates. "Would you like me to serve you?"

Macie smiled. "That sounds nice."

Landon filled her plate with a little of everything, then handed her the food and did the same with his plate. They ate for a few minutes as they watched the waves roll in.

Macie took a sip of her drink. "What gave you this nice idea? I didn't realize you were quite so…"

"Romantic? I actually had the idea while I was sick."

Her brows rose. "Really?"

"I dreamed of lying on the beach with you, holding your hand while we looked at the stars. I thought we should give it a try. I've never taken you on a real date, and I thought you might like to be wooed."

"Wooed. That's going back into the annals of time."

"Maybe so, but isn't that what a man does when he wants a woman?"

"What I do know is that I like it. Thank you." Macie leaned forward, and he met her for a tender kiss.

"You deserve it."

After they finished their meal, he cleaned things away and placed more wood on the fire. They stretched out on the blanket, and Landon took her hand and intertwined her fingers with his. She laid her head against his upper arm.

"Why did you decide to do this tonight?"

"You sure are full of questions. I heard there were supposed to be shooting stars tonight, and I thought this would be a perfect spot to watch them."

"I like your ideas."

They spent the next hour quietly looking at the stars. A few times one of them would point and call, "There's one."

Unable to stand having her so close but not in his arms, Landon rolled toward her. He kissed her bare shoulder before traveling over its ridge to nuzzle her neck on his way to her mouth. He was going to miss her more than he ever dreamed he would. "I really like you in this dress."

"I thought you might, since you asked me to wear it." There was such happiness in her voice.

"Always the smart mouth. But I'm thinking I might like you better without it." His lips took hers.

Macie smiled as she lounged on Landon's porch and drank her morning tea. He sat beside her on the small couch within touching distance. Last night had been wonderful. She was still floating with contentment.

They had made love on the beach and returned to his house to do so again in the middle of the night. He had been so tender and caring, and something about it had made her wonder if he'd been trying to tell her something. As if he wanted her to understand how special she was to him.

Now they were making a leisurely morning of it. She wished it could always be like this. Maybe she could talk Landon into staying. Get him to see that he could have a good life here with her.

"Macie?"

"Mmm?"

"That phone call yesterday when you were in my office was from DC."

Her stomach dropped. She turned to him. Was this the day she had been dreading? He would leave her once more. Only this time she'd known all along it would happen. She'd chosen this hurt and would have to deal with it. "When are you leaving?"

"In a couple of days."

A heaviness pressed down on her chest. She placed her mug on the coffee table and swung her legs round so she faced him. "That soon!"

He reached over and touched her arm. "We knew this was coming."

Yeah. But that didn't mean she had to like it. Or that she couldn't fight against it.

"Come with me," he said softly, almost as a plea. "I know you would be an asset to the World Health Organization."

She shook her head. "I can't do that."

"Why not? You haven't signed a contract here. You could stay behind long enough to train your replacement. We're great together. I don't want us to stop yet."

"I'm needed here. This is my home now."

Landon stood and glared down at her. "This is your hideout!"

"What?"

"You're here because you're afraid to go home. Afraid to face what you left behind."

She couldn't believe he was saying this to her. "That isn't true. And I don't even have a home to go to."

"You have a mother, brother and sister. Even a father. Who do you have here?" He waved his hand around.

"I have a lot of friends."

"Agreed, but they're not family. You live in a tiny rented house, and you work all the time. Every time someone needs something, you're there for them, but who's there for you?"

"You have been, but now you are leaving." She hadn't meant to sound so pitiful.

Landon eased back to the couch. "We both knew when I came that I wouldn't be staying long."

"I know." She looked at the floor. This was what she'd feared for weeks. What she'd chosen to ignore. "I told myself not to like you too much. But it didn't work."

He gave her a wry smile and reached for her hand. "If you come to Washington and don't want to work at World Health, with your skills you could work at one of the great hospitals around DC. You could still be making a difference but with me. Come on, Macie, think about it."

"I need to stay here and help the people of Saipan. One of us needs to stay to see that all those plans we've made happen." She saw him flinch. Her remark had hit home just as she'd hoped it would. He let go of her hand.

"I think you've already done your time." His words sounded like a judge giving his ruling. Firm and undeniable.

She lowered her chin and narrowed her eyes. "What're you talking about?"

"That you have been doing penitence for what your father did to all those people by being out here in the middle of nowhere, helping the forgotten."

"That's not true."

"Yeah, it is. Come on, Macie. You ran to Hawaii because of what your father did. You ran from Hawaii to here because of me, and now you're running from me again. There are only so many places you can go. All that *stuff*—" he tapped his chest "—is still with you. You can never outrun it because you carry it with you. Somewhere along the line you have to turn and face it. You're trying to make up for all your father's shortcomings by sacrificing your life."

"I'm not sacrificing anything." She glared at him.

"What about us?"

"What us? You don't really want an *us*. I've lived in a dreamworld before, and I refuse to do it again. What we've been doing here is playing house. What you have been offering me in Washington is more of the same. I don't want pretend. You said yourself that you could never give more, yet you are demanding I give up everything I have built to do just that."

"That's not true."

She looked at him for a moment. "For that matter, why can't you stay? Be the administrator. Better yet, practice medicine like you used to. We could use you here."

"I have a job waiting on me in DC that I've worked hard for years to get."

"Is it really what you want to do? To sit in an office pushing papers and telling people what's best to do for their patients, or would you rather be working with patients of your own? You've moved into what you're doing now because you needed the job to help your family, but is it really your dream? Haven't you left that behind?"

His mouth gaped as his stared at her. "I do important work."

"No one says you don't, but is it your dream? What you went into medicine to do?"

He just looked at her. She'd poked a tender spot. "A perfect world isn't possible."

"I'd be the first to agree with you on that. You took your job because it was a means to help your family, but your brother and sister are doing well—they even have families. But what about you? Isn't it time you get what you want? You could have a family that loves you if only you would let someone in. You don't have to be afraid of becoming your father."

"I'm not afraid."

"I think you are. You're better than him."

"It's not my father I'm afraid of becoming. It's my mother!" He all but shouted the words.

Macie couldn't have been more shocked. "Your mother?"

He stood again and paced the porch. "Yes! She loved my father so desperately that she destroyed her life and her children's lives when he left. I'm afraid that when I love, it will be so deeply that it could damage everyone around me if I lost it."

"So you're willing to keep me at arm's length for fear of loving me too much? That sounds like the perfect kind of love to me."

"That's not love. That's obsession."

"Landon, I think you need to figure out what you want." She stood as well.

"I want the job in Washington. I've worked for it and now is my chance. I can't just pass it up."

"You can't just pass it up *for me*. That's what you're not saying."

Landon gave her a stricken look. "I didn't say that."

"No, but that's what you mean. If you want me you have to stay here, which means that you have to give up the job and admit to loving me. Your attitude reminds me a lot of my father's. Whatever it takes for you to have what you want but not have to give anything back in return."

He jerked to a stop. "That's unfair. I would never hurt people the way your father did."

"I agree. You're a better person than him, but the principle is the same. Look, your work is in Washington and mine is here. Maybe we should just leave it at that. Say we had a good time while it lasted." She stood. Everything that needed saying had been said. "I'd like to go home now. We both need some space to think."

"Macie," he pleaded, stepping toward her.

"Please don't. I might fall apart if you touch me, and neither one of us needs that. The last thing I would want is for you to feel fenced in by me."

Landon sucked in a breath and backed away. "Macie, it isn't like that."

She pursed her lips. His inability to see the truth was a physical ache in her chest. "Isn't it?"

He had the good grace not to say anything.

This pain she carried was more than she had ever imagined. She wanted to run into his arms, hold him tight and have him say he would never let her go.

Landon turned toward the door. She quietly gathered her belongings, and then he took her home.

As she stepped out of the car, he asked, "Can I call you later today, or tomorrow?"

She shook her head. "No, I don't think that'll make anything easier, nor will it change our minds."

"I have the first flight out on Monday. Will you come see me off?"

She blinked a couple of times to control the moisture in her eyes. Shaking her head, she ran blindly for her front door, just managing to get inside before she burst into tears.

CHAPTER TEN

LANDON HAD BEEN in Washington, DC, for a week. Despite being busier than ever, he felt it had been the longest week of his life. He had left Saipan with a heavy heart when he should have been happy to be taking up the position he'd been working so hard to achieve.

He hadn't seen Macie—except once briefly at the hospital—since he had left her at her home. More than once he had picked up the phone to call her but had put it down again. She had needed space and he had given it to her. Still, it hurt that she hadn't wanted to spend what little time they had left together. He had hoped they would make plans to see each other, to maybe meet in Hawaii, but she had made no contact.

She hadn't come to the airport to see him off. He'd counted on her at least doing that. The chance to hold her one more time… But nothing. He had looked for her, but in the end he'd walked out to the plane with weighty steps. And then he'd become angry. He couldn't fathom why she wouldn't come with him. It had been years since she'd visited her family. Why couldn't she a least try? For him? For herself?

It wasn't until he had looked out the window as the plane took off that he saw her car parked on the side of the road, Macie standing beside it, looking up at the sky.

And at that moment, she had pulled his heart out and held it. He knew the love his mother had had for his father, the kind with the ability to take him to the highest high or the lowest low.

After a long flight and a night on the west coast, he had arrived in Washington, DC, to a hotel located a block from the World Health Organization office. He'd actually come home to nothing. He didn't own a house or a car. Because he was traveling all the time, he'd not seen a reason to buy either. He had nothing—emotionally or physically—in his life. How had he become such a loner? Had he been so busy protecting himself against being hurt that he had nothing to show for it?

He hadn't been alone in Saipan. He'd had Macie. What would it be like to come home to her every day? To their children? He'd never thought like that before. Right now, it sounded like bliss.

Over the past week he had spent a good deal of time urging board members to consider his suggestions for the hospital. He felt fairly positive about the proposal's chances, but the board needed an extra push for it to pass and he was going to suggest that they speak to both the Saipan representative to Congress and the governor to get a personal perspective.

Despite how busy he was, he couldn't get Macie out of his mind. During the day he survived, but it was the nights in his box of a room when he felt the loss in his life the most. He made a habit of working late so he didn't have to spend any more time there than necessary. Another week crept by, and the loneliness squeezed him like being crushed by a rock pile. Would he ever find that happiness again?

He had to make a trip to the Midwest to check on a project that he had worked on before going to Saipan.

That put him within hours of his sister's and brother's homes, which were in the same state.

He called Nancy and, as always, she made arrangements for the three of them to get together. Adam and his family would be coming to her house for dinner, and Landon would be the honored guest. He was looking forward to seeing his family again, but he also felt a twinge of nervousness. What would they think?

Both Nancy and Adam enveloped him in their arms. Finally, he felt a tiny amount of what he had experienced in Saipan, and the pressure in his chest eased some. This was love—the good, healthy type.

The evening meal was a rambunctious affair since his siblings both had small children. There were smiles all around and much laughter, and Landon enjoyed every bit of it. For the first time he was even envious. He wanted what they had.

The meal was at an end when Adam's wife announced she was putting the baby down for a nap. His brother-in-law took his child from Nancy's arms and mumbled something about watching a game on TV, leaving the siblings alone to catch up.

For a few moments, the three of them looked at each other, unsure, before they smiled and started talking at the same time. With the tension broken, they went back in time to when it was just the three of them against the world.

Adam said, "We need to do this more often."

Landon leaned back in his chair. "I couldn't agree more. It's great to see you both."

"So," Nancy asked as she studied Landon, "tell us, very important brother—" Adam huffed "—how have you been?"

"Fine."

Nancy's eyes narrowed. "You don't look fine."

When he had looked in the mirror that morning, he'd thought he looked the same as always. He just didn't feel the same.

"It must be jet lag. I've just gotten back from Saipan."

"That's right. I had to look that one up," she said.

"Yeah, me too," Adam added. "So what was in Saipan?"

Happiness. Macie. Everything. "A hospital that I was evaluating."

"And how did that go?" His sister refilled his glass.

"Overall, I think it was positive. There are still some decisions to make but I think it'll be very successful."

"And you'll be getting this new job?" Adam crossed his arms on the table, giving Landon his full attention.

"Yes, I'll be Director of the World Health Organization."

"Impressive." His brother nodded thoughtfully.

"And living in Washington?" Nancy asked.

"Yes. I'll be staying in one place finally." Somehow that idea had more appeal than ever before.

"Great. We'll get to see you more often. We won't have to chase you down all the time." She gave him a pointed look. "For a man who has a big new job, you sure don't look very happy about it."

He didn't feel it either. "It's a great job. I can make a difference."

"That's good." Nancy didn't sound like she really believed him.

Landon could always talk to his brother and sister. What they had lived through had brought them closer; they understood him. Despite the fact that they didn't see each other often, they knew each other well. They always slipped back to where they'd left off.

Nancy continued to give him an unwavering look. One that reminded him too much of their mother. Landon shifted in his chair.

"I've always known when something was bothering you."

She had. Landon looked at Adam, who just grinned at him.

"I know that look. You've met a woman!" Nancy said it like she'd just made a difficult puzzle piece fit in.

Landon groaned.

His brother slapped his hand on the table. "It's about damn time."

"So when do we meet her?" Nancy demanded.

His lips tightened and he looked away. "I don't think you will."

"What! Why?" His sister all but squealed.

Landon explained what had happened between him and Macie. He finished with "She wouldn't come with me."

"Did you mention to her that you're in love with her?"

As if a lock had sprung, his brain engaged. He was in love with Macie, and he'd left her halfway around the world. What had he been thinking? He hadn't been.

"You didn't know," Nancy said in disbelief. "Or if you did, you didn't tell her."

"Landon, I know that Mom and Dad's marriage nearly wrecked us," Adam offered, "but that's no reason not to have someone to love."

"I, uh…"

His sister placed her hand over his. "Landon, you had a harder time than we did because you were the oldest and you thought you had to take care of us, and everything you've done since—including your jobs—has been about what we needed. Have you ever thought about what *you* want? We appreciate everything you've done for us, but we're all settled now and we would never want you to give up your life for us."

"I haven't given up anything." Landon didn't like the turn the conversation had taken.

"Yes, you did," Adam insisted. "We weren't so young that we didn't know where the money was coming from."

"And you don't have to be like our parents. Just because they had a horrible marriage doesn't mean you have to. Or that you would be as uncaring as Dad or as needy as Mom. We can be our own people." Nancy nodded toward Adam. "If we took a chance, so can you."

Had he been doing those things? Projecting his parents' problems on to himself, on to the women he dated, on to Macie? If anything, she had proved herself to be nothing like his mother.

"We always knew, and we love you for it, but it's time for you to decide what you want and go after it. Time for you to live your life. Time to find happiness." His sister patted his hand.

Could he give up everything he had worked for and go back to Saipan? "It's too late."

"It's never too late to tell someone you love them," she assured him.

He looked at Adam then Nancy. "I love you guys."

Macie watched the plane disappear into the sky, taking Landon with it. The beautiful sunny day was in complete opposition to the gloomy tempest of emotions within her. The love of her life had left her again, and this time she'd known it was going to happen and still had been unable to prevent it.

She climbed into her car, placed her hands over her face and sobbed. Had she done the right thing? Or had she been doing exactly what he'd accused her of: hiding?

For the first time since she had come to Saipan, she called in and took a day off. She drove out to the place where she and Landon had gone on their beach picnic. It had been the best of nights and the worst of mornings. That had been only two days ago, but it felt like forever. She'd missed him the moment he'd left her at her house. She'd needed to think. He'd not called, and she'd not tried to get in contact with him. Was it going to change anything if she did? Hadn't they picked their corners and made their decisions?

She walked to the beach and sat down to watch the waves roll in. How had she come to this? Because she'd let her emotions take over. She'd opened her heart and Landon had walked in. From their time in Hawaii she'd known he had the power to make her love him and she was well aware of how it felt to have someone you loved disappoint you.

When the sun started setting and the hunger pains didn't pass, she went home. She prepared her supper but ate only a few bites. Deciding sleep would give her some relief from the pain, she went to bed. But she was disappointed. All she could think about was how she missed Landon's arms around her and his warm body next to hers. She tossed and turned until the sky turned pink, and then she dressed for work. Maybe there she could find some peace.

But she didn't, and the rest of the week went much as the first day had. She became even more sleep deprived, and her colleagues began to look at her oddly. She'd snapped at a number of them, and Tatiana gave her a wide berth. Even in the darkest days of her father's trial she'd never been this miserable.

Why had she let this happen? She should have protected herself better.

But what was done was done, and now she had to figure out how to survive. Was that really what she wanted, to just survive? Wasn't that what she'd been doing for the last eight years? Surviving by hiding. If she wanted to deserve Landon, she had to do better than that. When she went after him—which she planned to—she had to be worthy of him.

She'd accused Landon of needing to clear up stuff in his life. Didn't she need to address her past as well? She hadn't seen her family in years, and it was time for her to face what her father had done head-on.

With weeks of vacation time stored up, she could go get her life in order, and then she would find Landon and tell him how she felt. Even if he didn't want her, it was time she reenter the world.

She couldn't leave the hospital without making arrangements and finding a replacement. If Landon still wanted her, she would return to pack up and move to Washington so she could be with him.

It took her a little over a week to get her affairs in order at work and to make phone calls home. When she spoke to her mother and said she was coming for a visit, her mother broke down in tears.

"I'll be waiting for you at the airport," her mother said.

"You don't have to do that, Mom."

"I want to. I can't wait to see you."

In that moment Macie was confident she was doing the right thing, regardless of what happened with Landon.

"Your brother and sister will be so excited. I'll ask

them to come for the weekend. I can't believe I'll have all my children under one roof again."

Macie had to admit she was looking forward to seeing her family. If she'd been asked a few weeks ago if she would be seeing them, she wouldn't have thought it possible.

"How's Daddy?" It was the first time she'd ever asked about her father.

"He's fine. Just a little older and more tired."

Macie had to admire her mother. She had stayed by his side—that was true love. Would she do that if Landon were in prison? Love meant love in good times or bad. Thick or thin.

"Do you think he'd like to see me?"

There was quiet on her mother's end then a sniffle. "He would love that."

"Could you please make the arrangements?"

"I will," her mother assured her.

"I'll see you soon, Mom. I love you." Macie looked out the window of her house. She really had placed her life on hold when she'd come here.

Her visit with her family a few days later was wonderful—a little uncomfortable at first but heartwarming in the end. At the airport, her mother had pulled her into a hug so tight that Macie had found it difficult to breathe. As they'd approached her mom's small house in a subdivision, Macie could see a large sign across the front door that read Welcome Home Macie.

Her chest had tightened. She should have been better to her mother—she wasn't the one who had done anything wrong. All that fell on her father.

It had been wonderful to reconnect with her siblings and their families over the weekend, and she'd regretted the time she'd missed with them, especially her nieces and nephews.

After her visit with her family, her phone rang Monday morning. "Hello?"

"Macie Beck?"

"Yes."

"This is Dr. Larry Fitzgerald with the World Health Organization."

Her hand shook. Had something happened to Landon?

"We'd like to invite you to come to Washington to share with the board your view on the proposed changes to the hospital and what we can do to help."

Really? Why wasn't Landon calling her? "Did Dr. Cochran ask you to call me?"

"No. He's currently on assignment out of town."

Oh. A pain shot through her. She hadn't told him she was coming to the States, so there was no reason to expect he would be sitting in Washington waiting for her.

The man continued. "Will you come? We would certainly pay your expenses."

"Yes." She had to. It mattered to the hospital. It mattered to Landon's future for the project to go well.

"When could you be here?"

"Would the end of the week do?"

"So soon?" The shock was clear in the man's voice.

"I'm actually in the States currently, in the Chicago area."

"Good, good. I'll be back in touch to finalize arrangements. Please plan on Friday."

"I will. Thank you for this opportunity."

"Thank you, Ms. Beck."

The next day, she drove to the minimum-security prison outside Chicago to visit her father. Her stomach was a jumble of nerves. She had to grip the steering wheel to keep her hands from shaking. If she wasn't careful, she'd lose her lunch.

She had to wait in a large room with tables populated by other visitors meeting with their loved ones while two men stood guard on each side of the room. Her father came in wearing an orange jumpsuit and looking much older than she remembered. Life had beat him down.

He smiled, but it was an uncertain one as he approached. "Macie."

She thought to stand to greet him or to hug him, but she couldn't bring herself to do either. She didn't know how to respond, so she just nodded.

"You have grown into such a beautiful woman. I almost didn't recognize you." He took a seat across from her. "How have you been?"

"I've been fine." She twisted her fingers together.

"Working as a nurse in Saipan, your mother has proudly told me."

"Yes." This was her father and they were strangers. They stared at each other for a long moment before Macie blurted out, "Why did you do it? Why?"

He looked at the table then back at her. "Because I didn't think I would get caught."

"But all those people you hurt?"

"For that I am sorry."

At least he could say that, but it didn't bring their life savings back. "I have hated you."

"For that I'm sorry as well. Please keep your voice down."

One of the guards watched them with interest.

"You do know that I've been gone all these years because I couldn't face people. The press hounded me, made my life a misery." All the bitterness flowed out of her as she said all the things she had not articulated to him before.

"All I can say is that I'm sorry."

"That's not enough," Macie hissed.

"I know, but that's all I have to give."

Macie just looked at him. What more did she have to say to him?

"Look, honey—"

"Don't call me that!" Macie snapped. Now she knew why she had stayed away.

Her father sighed and reached a hand across the table. "I can't give you what you want. The best I can do is to tell you I love you and ask you for your forgiveness."

She studied his hand but didn't reach out to him. It was still too raw. "I love you too, Dad. I forgive you—not for you, but for me. I have to let it go so I can move on."

He nodded.

"I think I need to go," Macie said.

"I understand."

Macie couldn't get to the car fast enough. She wished Landon was there to hold her. Gripping the steering wheel, she leaned her head against it, inhaling deeply and then releasing her breath slowly. She'd had no idea what to expect from her father, but she felt better for visiting at least and she'd gotten some of her anger out. A weight she'd had no idea she'd been carrying was gone.

How she wanted to see Landon. Would he be in Washington when she got there? If he wasn't, she'd wait.

Landon entered the boardroom in the World Health Organization building. The space had been rearranged so that the board sat in a semicircle of desks with chairs in the front, a long table between them with a microphone on it. Behind them, on either side of an aisle, were rows of chairs for those who were attending the hearing. This was a public event, so it often drew interested parties and the media.

It had been only the afternoon before when he had checked his messages and learned that he was expected to appear before the board and that Macie would be testifying as well. Since he had been out of town longer than he had originally planned visiting family and had not picked up his messages in the last twenty-four hours he'd just learned of the arrangements. To say he'd been surprised would be an understatement.

Macie was here in Washington. He would see her! After his conversation with Adam and Nancy, he had been convinced he had to return to Saipan, had to go after Macie, had to try again. If she wouldn't come here, then he would go there. It was time to quit living in the past and start building his future, and Macie was his future.

Despite his efforts to arrive early, he had been waylaid by a couple of phone calls and then stopped in the hallway by a colleague who wanted to discuss a project they had worked on during the last year. By the time he reached the room, it was filling with people. He searched for Macie; his body sensed her and he imagined if he inhaled deeply, he would be able to pick up her unique scent. Seconds later he spotted her, speaking to someone at the front of the room.

His heart came close to thumping out of his chest. Macie had never looked lovelier, nor more desirable. Or was that because he'd missed her so much? She wore a simple pale pink dress with a black blazer. A gold necklace hung around her neck, and her hair swung freely about her face. His hands ached to touch its silkiness.

Another person stopped him, but even as his colleague spoke, his attention kept returning to Macie. He noticed she kept looking over her shoulder as if she were expecting someone. Was she looking for him? Warmth filled his chest at the idea. He hoped she was as anxious to see him as he was to see her.

The president of the board spoke into the microphone in front of his chair. "We need to get this meeting started. Please take your seats."

As Landon excused himself from the conversation and walked to the front of the room, he watched as the woman Macie had been speaking to escorted her to a chair at the table facing the board. Before she sat, Macie pulled a folder out of the bag she carried.

He had just slid into the seat beside her when the chairman called the meeting to order. This wasn't the way he'd wanted their reunion to go, but under the circumstances it couldn't be helped. They would talk afterward. He would see to that.

Macie's eyes widened with awareness, and a look of pleasure filled them.

"Hey," he said well away from the microphone. Instead of speaking to her, what he really wanted to do was grab her in his arms and kiss her until both of them couldn't breathe. He settled for looking deep into her eyes.

"Hi. I was told you might not be here."

"And you thought I wouldn't show up to see you?" Landon searched her face. He had missed her so much.

"I hoped you would." Her words were soft and unsure.

Landon inhaled her heavenly scent—fresh air and coconut—and he held her look until the chairman called the meeting to order.

The chairman introduced the board and Macie, and Landon as well. The chairman then spoke directly to Macie. "Ms. Beck, I hope you don't mind if we tape this hearing. We'd like to have it for review purposes." He indicated the camera in the corner.

The tension in Macie came off her in waves. She stared ahead. Landon wanted to reach for her, knowing how she felt about cameras, but he couldn't do that, so he pushed a piece of paper off the table and leaned over to pick it up. Coming close to her ear, he said, "You can do this. I'm right here beside you."

Her gaze met his and she blinked. "That's fine," she said into the microphone.

"I understand that you'd like to make a statement," the chairman said.

"I would." She opened the folder.

Macie proceeded to give a statement that clearly came from her heart—how she felt about Saipan, the people and the hospital was evident in her voice. She finished with "In conclusion, I believe this is a sound plan and could make a difference in people's lives."

"Dr. Cochran, before we start the questions, is there anything you would like to add?"

Landon leaned toward the microphone. "No, sir. I think Miss Beck has more than adequately covered the points."

Macie looked at him, and he gave her a reassuring nod.

"Now, if any of the board has any questions for Ms. Beck and Dr. Cochran, this is the time to ask," the chairman said.

Over the next hour, Landon and Macie fielded questions about the hospital, the plans, updates on equipment and, most important, how much funding would be required.

Landon believed the meeting was winding down when one of the board members said, "All of this sounds good, but I'm still not convinced. You have both expressed your belief that it's the leadership going forward that will make the difference. I'd be more likely to vote yes if a committed administrator was in place."

Another board member spoke up. "I agree. Before we commit to the funding, shouldn't we seek to secure an administrator who commits to staying at least five years and who will be responsible for seeing these projects through? Otherwise, I don't see these plans being carried out to their fullest potential."

A couple of the other board members nodded. Macie's dejected look clearly said she was afraid their work had been wasted, her dreams gone. Landon wanted to make her dreams come true. Always.

"Sir, if I were to take the position as administrator of the Saipan Hospital until one could be found who would sign a five-year contract and be trained on the long-term strategy, would the board consider supporting the changes immediately?"

Macie's quick inhale of breath plainly revealed her shock. She looked at him in disbelief, her mouth gaping. She pushed the microphone back. "What are you doing? What about your new position?"

He smiled. "I've decided that some things are more important."

"What things?" she whispered.

"You."

The chairman cleared his throat, bringing their attention back to the room.

"How would the board feel about that arrangement? Under Dr. Cochran's leadership I think it would be a workable plan." The chairman looked at the other board members who had voiced their concerns. They all nodded agreement.

"I think we have all we need for now. Ms. Beck, thank

you for making such a long journey. This hearing is adjourned."

There was a shuffling of feet as everyone stood.

Macie couldn't believe what Landon had just done. What type of man gave up his entire career just like that? One completely different from her father, that was for sure. If she hadn't already been in love with Landon, she was now.

She turned to him and grasped his hand. "You don't have to do this. You don't have to give up all you've been working for."

"I'm not giving up anything. I'm just postponing it."

A man placed his hand on Landon's shoulder, interrupting their conversation. "Landon, if you're serious about returning to Saipan, then we need to talk."

"I'm serious, sir. Macie, this is my boss and friend, Dr. Russell."

"Hello," Macie said.

The man glanced at their hands and smiled. "I think our discussion can wait until tomorrow morning. Why don't you take Ms. Beck out to lunch and show her some of DC while she's here?"

"Thank you, I will." Landon offered the man his hand. "Thank you, sir."

"Ms. Beck, thank you for coming. You are an impressive and persuasive woman."

As Dr. Russell walked off, Landon said, "Let's get out of here before we're interrupted again. We need to talk."

He led her outside into the bright spring sunlight. Taking her hand, Landon started down the sidewalk.

"Where are we going?" Macie walked beside him.

"To a little café I know where we won't be disturbed.

I'd rather take you to my hotel room, but we wouldn't get any talking done there."

"Landon?" She pulled on his hand and stopped.

He did as well and looked down at her. "What?"

"I love you. I shouldn't have let you leave Saipan without me."

He cupped her cheek and looked into her eyes. "I love you too, and I should have told you that."

Coming up onto her toes, she met Landon for a kiss more perfect than she could have ever imagined. It wasn't until someone honked their horn that they drew apart, laughing.

Landon took her hand again and turned back the way they had come.

"Where are we going now?" She had to hurry to keep up with him.

"To my hotel."

She grinned as she tightened her grip on his hand. "I thought you were hungry and wanted to talk."

"I am hungry. For you. And we've already said what needed to be said."

A heat filled her chest that flowed right to her center.

Landon whisked her inside a stately old hotel, through the lobby and into the elevator. There he pulled her into his arms and kissed her until her knees buckled. When the doors opened, he guided her down the hall to a door, unlocked it and pushed it open. She stepped inside, but Landon remained outside.

"Aren't you coming in?" Panic filled her. Had he changed his mind?

"In a sec." He took a deep breath.

She watched him, confused.

Landon looked shaken. "I love you so much and have

missed you so much that I'm afraid I might hurt you with how much I want you."

Macie's heart swelled. She tugged him to her. "I'll take my chances."

He scooped her into his arms, and she giggled as he tumbled her onto the bed.

Blissful, precious hours later, they sat in bed wearing plush hotel bathrobes while sharing a meal Landon had ordered from room service.

"Landon, I appreciate your offer to be the administrator, but I don't want you to feel like you have to."

"I might have said it in the heat of the moment, but I would have never done so unless I thought it was what I wanted. I was happy in Saipan. With you, with the people, with the work. I found—" he met her eyes "—more than one thing I had lost. I want to work with patients again, and I was coming back anyway. To you."

"When I got the call to come to DC, I was already in the States."

"You were?" He lifted a strawberry to her lips.

She bit it and swallowed. "Mmm… What you said about me hiding out got me to thinking that I couldn't always live my life that way. It had been too long since I had seen my family, so I came to visit them. I even went to see my father."

Landon ran his hand over her hair. "I should have been with you when you went to see your father."

She gave him a wry smile. "Thank you for that."

"How did it go?"

She bit her bottom lip for a moment. "I'm not sure. He seemed glad to see me. I confronted him about some things."

"And?"

"He said he was sorry, but I'm still not convinced he

means it." Landon gave her a look of sympathy. "Anyway, I was planning to come here to see you when the chairman called."

"I didn't know you were here until yesterday afternoon." He played with her fingertips.

She grinned. "Were you surprised?"

"Pleasantly." He moved the food out of the way and pulled her to him, kissing her. "Anxiously." He nipped at her neck. "Hungrily." He kissed her palm. "And happily."

She put a hand on his chest. "Seriously, Landon. I don't want you to give up your promotion for me and my wants."

"I'm not giving up anything. I'm gaining a life, a job I love and, best of all…you. I hope you didn't give up your job. You're going to need it when you return."

"You said something about postponing your job. What do you mean?"

"I'm going to ask Dr. Russell if I can continue to be paid through the organization. That will help the hospital financially, and it'll also leave the door open for me to be considered for promotions in the future."

"Oh, Landon, that's too much." She wrapped her arms around his neck and kissed him.

When they broke apart, he said, "There's more.

"When there's an administrator in place who can handle the day-to-day issues, I'm going back to patient care part-time. I've missed it. I'll start working immediately in the ER on weekends when you are there. That'll sharpen up my skills, and I'm also going to stipulate that the organization pay for two airline tickets home twice a year. We need to visit our families. Sometimes you have to leave paradise."

Joy filled Macie. It all sounded so wonderful. "Do you think Dr. Russell will agree to everything?"

"I do." Landon's look turned serious. "I have a question for you."

"What's that?"

"Will you marry me?"

"Oh, Landon." She gave him a questioning look.

"Well?" He sounded worried.

"Are you sure that's what you want? I know how you feel about that type of commitment."

"Married or not, you're still my life. I love you so much already it almost takes my breath away. Nothing you or I do will ever change that."

"Yes. Yes. I'll marry you." She threw herself into his arms. "With you I'll always be in paradise."

* * * * *